We acknowledge
the traditional owners of the land
on which we live and learn.
We pay our respects to the Elders,
past and present,
and we thank them for taking care of country
over countless generations.

PLAYGROUND

Listening to stories
from country
and from inside the heart

Compiled by Nadia Wheatley

Illustration and design: Ken Searle   Indigenous consultant: Jackie Huggins

This edition published in 2011

Every effort has been made to trace the original
source of copyright material contained in this book.
The publishers would be pleased to hear from
copyright holders of any errors or omissions.

Copyright in text, photographs and artwork
remains with the original copyright holders
as noted in Acknowledgements pp. 94–6.

Introductory text and compilation of material: © Nadia Wheatley
Illustrations: © Ken Searle

Design by Ken Searle
Cover artwork and design by Ken Searle
Computer design by Jo Hunt
Set in Berkeley Book

Allen & Unwin   Phone: (61 2) 8425 0100
83 Alexander St   Fax: (61 2) 9906 2218
Crows Nest NSW 2065   Email: info@allenandunwin.com
Australia   Web: www.allenandunwin.com

A Cataloguing-in-Publication entry is available from the National Library of Australia
www.trove.nla.gov.au

ISBN 978 1 74237 097 2

This book was printed in January 2011 by Imago at Star Standard Industries Pty Ltd,
8/10 Gul Lane, Jurong Town, Jurong Industrial Estate, Singapore 629409
10 9 8 7 6 5 4 3 2 1

Teachers notes available from www.allenandunwin.com

A note on the editing

Ever since I was young, I have loved stories about other people's childhoods.

Over the last couple of decades, I have been fascinated to read accounts of childhood which have appeared in the memoirs written by Aboriginal people or recorded by them in the form of oral history. While these narratives make up an enormous heritage of Australian history, they are mostly not published in a way that is accessible to the general reader – let alone the young reader.

And so, believing that many Australians would be interested in this material if it were made available, I decided to combine excerpts from some of these publications with some new oral history, including interviews with young Indigenous people who are growing up in the twenty-first century.

As a non-Indigenous person, my role is that of compiler and editor. I have been very fortunate to have Dr Jackie Huggins as my Indigenous consultant, to act as my adviser, safety net, and (as Jackie herself puts it) 'critical friend'. Naturally, I take responsibility for any mistakes in the way the material has been put together.

I have provided short introductions to the book's topics and its contributors, but it is the stories themselves that contain the meaning. Although the subject matter has been loosely arranged to follow the stages in a child's learning journey, readers are welcome to dip in at random. The culture that underlies these narratives is holistic: everything connects, no matter which way you come at it. As my friend Linda Anderson Tjonggarda, from Papunya, once summed up for me: 'It all goes back to the land. It always goes back to the land.'

While I have tried to include accounts and images from across the continent, and from a wide number of language groups and nations, I have barely skimmed the surface. With only eighty pages available and no funding for research or travel, I could not even try to represent everything.

Apologies: This book contains some stories and photos of Aboriginal people who have passed away. Including this material allows their history to be read by future generations. However, there is always the possibility that someone might see a name or an image that could cause distress. So I ask Aboriginal and Torres Strait Islander readers to proceed with caution, and to accept my apologies for any sadness that may be caused.

For some of the people in this anthology, English is an unfamiliar language, forced on them by government officials, bosses, missionaries and unsympathetic schoolteachers. It would have been disrespectful of me to change the words used by the storytellers, and so I have left the accounts as they appear in their original source.

A brief glossary is provided on page 97, but many Aboriginal words are best understood in context. In the oral history passages, a translation is usually given in brackets after the Aboriginal word. My only editorial change has been to standardise the English spelling of the names of Aboriginal languages and nations, to avoid confusing readers with variant spellings. While I have done my best to follow the usage preferred in communities today, I apologise if any communities or individuals prefer a different spelling.

Thanks: I would like to thank the many people in community organisations and schools who helped me to get in touch with contributors or permitted me to talk with students. My thanks also go to Jackie Huggins. Without her support and her wisdom, I would not have dared take on this job. I would also like to acknowledge the team of Elders, teachers and students with whom Ken Searle and I worked at Papunya School in the late 1990s – especially Emma Nungarrayi, Linda Anderson Tjonggarda, Charlotte Phillipus, Punata Stockman, Mary Malbunka, Diane de Vere and Jenny Wilson. Thank you for setting Ken and me on this journey.

Finally, my heartfelt thanks go to the 111 Aboriginal and Torres Strait Islander contributors and their families who have allowed their words and artwork to be included in this book. Every time I read these stories, I feel very privileged. I hope that this book helps other non-Indigenous Australians to start learning how to listen to stories that come from country and from inside the heart.

Kala palya!

Nadia Wheatley

CONTENTS

Introduction

Playing... listening... learning... helping... sharing... having fun... showing respect... caring for country...

These are some of the things that the children of this land have been doing for thousands upon thousands of years.

In traditional time, kids didn't have to set off from home in the morning in order to go to school. The whole country was a vast outdoor classroom, which contained everything that the First Children needed to know. The land was also their playground.

As kids journeyed with their families from place to place, it was often impossible to tell the difference between playing and learning. School was home, and home was the traditional country where the family had been living since the Law began. The teachers were parents, grandparents, aunties, uncles, cousins, sisters and brothers. The whole community took on the responsibility for the education of a child.

When large groups of people met together, kids learned new lessons through watching the ceremonies that enacted the stories about the ancestral beings who had set down the rules for how people should behave towards each other and the land.

Just as there was Law for every aspect of adult life, so children had their own Law, which was passed down from generation to generation. While this set out the rules of the games that they played and the words of their songs and stories, the Law also said that big kids had to look after little kids and show them what to do. Because children cared for each other and knew their own country, they could be given a great deal of freedom to go off and play, without adult supervision.

In the bush, there were trees to climb and creeks to swim in. There was great cover for games of hide-and-seek, and plenty of open space for ball games. Cubbies were built at every campsite, and kids lit their own small fires if they wanted to cook themselves a snack. When the family moved on to a new home, the toys went back into the playground, to be ready for the next visit.

Since European people have come to Australia, Aboriginal children have taken on some new ways of getting an education and having fun. Yet whether they live on a remote outstation or in a busy city, they continue a way of learning that comes from observing and copying, helping and sharing, and listening to the stories of country which their families have been telling since the old days.

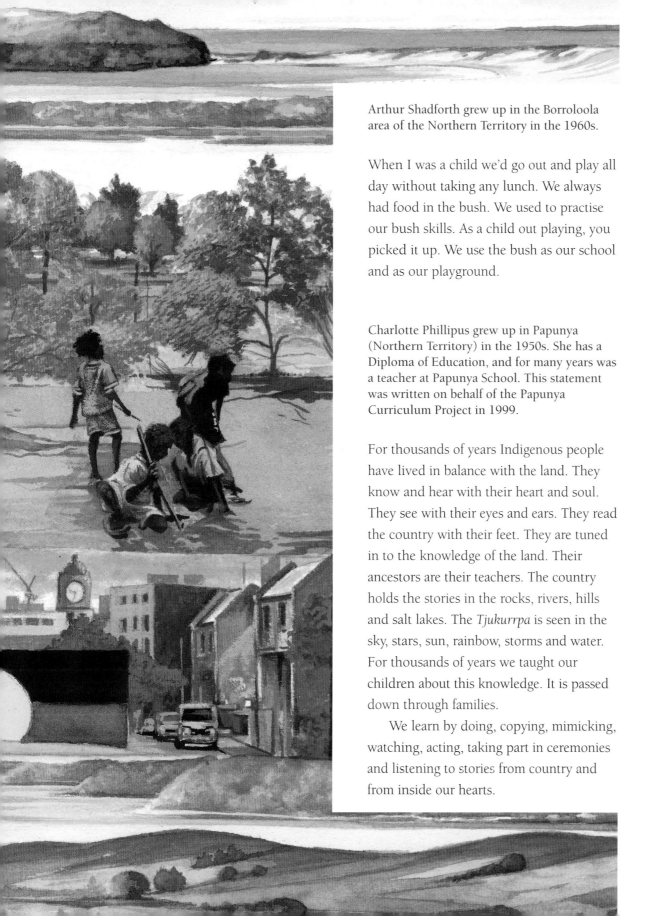

Arthur Shadforth grew up in the Borroloola area of the Northern Territory in the 1960s.

When I was a child we'd go out and play all day without taking any lunch. We always had food in the bush. We used to practise our bush skills. As a child out playing, you picked it up. We use the bush as our school and as our playground.

Charlotte Phillipus grew up in Papunya (Northern Territory) in the 1950s. She has a Diploma of Education, and for many years was a teacher at Papunya School. This statement was written on behalf of the Papunya Curriculum Project in 1999.

For thousands of years Indigenous people have lived in balance with the land. They know and hear with their heart and soul. They see with their eyes and ears. They read the country with their feet. They are tuned in to the knowledge of the land. Their ancestors are their teachers. The country holds the stories in the rocks, rivers, hills and salt lakes. The *Tjukurrpa* is seen in the sky, stars, sun, rainbow, storms and water. For thousands of years we taught our children about this knowledge. It is passed down through families.

We learn by doing, copying, mimicking, watching, acting, taking part in ceremonies and listening to stories from country and from inside our hearts.

Joe Brown is a Special Adviser for the Kimberley Aboriginal Law and Culture Centre in Western Australia. Like Charlotte Phillipus, he talks of the importance of the traditional way of learning through the stories of country. While Charlotte uses the word '*Tjukurrpa*' for the Law, in Joe's language the word is '*Ngarrangkarni*'.

All the old people know the meaning of the story for their own country. People believe in that story and follow that story from the time we call *Ngarrangkarni*. Non-Aboriginal people say Dreamtime.

Ngarrangkarni is just like 'In the beginning'. Just like the Gospel has the story of Adam and Eve, Aboriginal people have stories about land and animals and people from the beginning when the world was soft. These stories teach you everything. How to live in the country and how to respect each other. These stories are the Law. They tell you about important places we have to look after... If you break the Law you will get punished.

We have to teach all the story from the *Ngarrangkarni* to our kids. When people start to learn that story they keep Law and Culture strong and we feel *wirriya* (happy)...

It is our right to be able to teach our kids songs, stories and ceremonies about our country. Our Law and Culture is alive and strong.

Where babies come from

In traditional time, Aboriginal people believed that a spirit came into a woman when she became pregnant. This meant that every child was sacred.

When a woman felt a baby first stir inside her womb, she made sure to remember whatever she saw at that moment, because she knew that there was a special connection between her child and that type of animal or plant. In Aboriginal languages there are many different words for this relationship, but in English it is sometimes called a totem. People know that their special plant or animal will always look after them, like a guardian, and they in turn have a duty to look after their protector.

While the spirit-totem was important, so was the place where the unborn baby first let its mother know that it was alive and kicking. By being conceived or born in a place, children owned the right to share in the ancestral Dreaming or Law of that place. As well as having their own Dreamings, children inherited the Dreamings of their parents and grandparents.

There are many Aboriginal children today who know their traditional country and their ancestral Dreamings, even if they live in communities and townships.

Läklak Marika grew up in the community of Yirrkala in north-east Arnhem Land (Northern Territory). She tells the story of her conception-spirit, which came from a coastal area called Yalangbara, to the south of Yirrkala.

The word *gäthu* is a Yolngu word that a man and his sister use for the man's child. In English, we do not have a word for this relationship.

I was born at Yirrkala near the beach in 1943, but before that my spirit came from Yalangbara. My father, Mawalan Marika, and his brother were at Yalangbara. They caught a lot of fish and the next day they went out in a canoe and caught a green-back turtle. Then they took it back to land and ate it.

When they were sleeping, my father saw his sister in a dream. She was carrying me. I was wearing feathered armbands and waistbands. My father's sister said to him, 'This is our *gäthu*. You know that fish and turtle? She gave it to us.' My father said, 'All right, we got returns from her, rations from her. I'm glad for my daughter.'

Then my father woke up and he told my mother, 'I dreamt about that girl. You know that fish and turtle? That's from our daughter. This is the spirit landing for her.'

Rankin Deveraux is a member of the Mak Mak people, whose homeland is the Wagait floodplain of the Northern Territory. Every Mak Mak person knows their *mirr*, and this spirit-totem links them in a unique way to their world.

My [traditional] name is Ngalgal and that's my Dreaming, that hill. How I got my name was my uncle and Dad were up there waiting for the tide to go out and a big black saltwater croc popped up, and when they got back to camp they told Nana and Nana asked Mum if she was pregnant and Mum said yes, she was. So that's how I got my name from that place – Ngalgal – over there.

Young Mak Mak man Rankin Deveraux, photographed in 2002.

Goobalathaldin (Dick Roughsey) was a member of the Lardil people, owners of Mornington Island and other islands in the Gulf of Carpentaria. He has another way of describing the conception process.

Our old people believe that baby spirits live in the small bubbling holes that can be seen along the seashore at low tide. If a man is out hunting for fish or turtles and has good luck, such as the easy capture of a big fish, turtle or stingray, he knows that a baby spirit has entered into that fish or turtle and is looking for a mother. The man takes the fish or turtle home and gives some to his wife to eat, so that the baby spirit enters the woman. The woman already has an egg like a turtle egg inside her; it is made up of semen and menstrual blood. The baby spirit breaks into this egg and so grows inside the mother until it is born.

Joshua Booth is an Elder of the Martu people, who now mostly live in the communities of Punmu and Parnngurr, in the Karlamilyi National Park (Western Australia). Here Joshua speaks of a great Creator Spirit, whom he does not name.

Martu people come from *Jukurtani* (Dreamtime). He created the earth, the Martu people and the animals. He formed four kinship groups... so that the people can be carried on straight. He taught people what's good, what's bad, what's to eat, what's not to eat. He taught people where the waterholes are, which ones are salty and which ones are not...

He taught people that when their family members die they go back to the Dreamtime and can come back as someone else's baby. Sometimes Martu will see that person in a dream before they come back.

Arrernte Elder Wenten Rubuntja has said: 'All kids born at the Alice Springs Hospital are *yipirinya* kids.' In his view all children, whether Indigenous or non-Indigenous, who are born in Alice Springs inherit the Dreaming of the *yipirinya* (caterpillar), whose hills encircle the town. Here he tells the story of the *yipirinya* to two local boys.

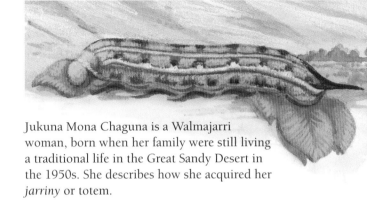

Jukuna Mona Chaguna is a Walmajarri woman, born when her family were still living a traditional life in the Great Sandy Desert in the 1950s. She describes how she acquired her *jarriny* or totem.

Near Mantarta is a smooth sand-hill called Lantimangu. It's a place where spirit children live. When a husband and wife walk near there, one of the spirits thinks, 'I'll go to them. I'll make them a mother and father.' One time my parents got a lot of edible gum from desert nut trees that were growing all around there, on a flat down from Lantimangu. That night my father had a dream and saw a child standing behind him, but when he turned round it disappeared. Next day he said to his wife, 'This gum might be the *jarriny* for our baby.' He had a feeling about it. Then my mother knew she was expecting me, and so my spirit comes from that sand-hill called Lantimangu.

Welcoming the new arrival

When babies were newborn, they were often gently rubbed in the sand of Mother Earth, to cleanse their skin.

After a day or two, or sometimes a few weeks, the mothers and aunties held a ceremony to welcome the new arrival, and leaves were burned to make a fragrant smoke. In some Aboriginal communities there is still a smoking ceremony when mothers and new infants come out of hospital and return to their home.

Peggy Patrick, Mona Ramsay and Shirley Purdie from Warmun Aboriginal Community in Western Australia describe welcoming a baby with water as the mother gives birth.

The water we use to sprinkle on the girl is water from the Dreamtime for us (*Mantha*)... The baby feels welcome and wants to come to us even before it is born. This is like baptism for you. In Aboriginal way it is welcoming someone and giving them a blessing to live.

Arrernte Elder Douglas Abbott describes the smoking ceremony that took place after his brother was born in their traditional land around the Finke River, to the south-west of Alice Springs, in the 1950s.

When my young brother was born, Mum went over, and all the women and I went with them and other kids, and they dug this hole and made this fire and got these branches of a certain type of bush, called *poondi*, broom bush white man's name. They made a thick smoke and my mother is rolling in it with the baby. She's cleaning her soul after birth, getting that thing strong with the smoke...

See, in the old days, when women gave birth, they stayed at this special place called *Iwekere*, alongside the river, where the baby was born. They'd camp there till the women had gone through that smoke ceremony, then they'd stay out there for maybe three weeks, a very long time, till that woman really heals. The father could only go to a certain point, halfway; no man was allowed to go to that [birthing place]. The old grandmother would know when [the woman] is ready to come back.

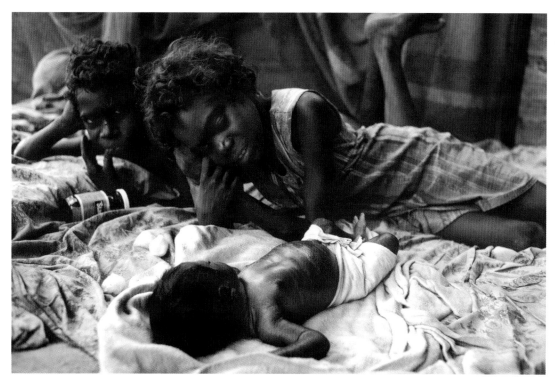

A new baby is welcomed in Arnhem Land (Northern Territory) in the late 1970s.

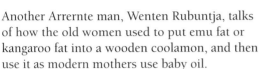

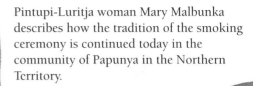

Pintupi-Luritja woman Mary Malbunka describes how the tradition of the smoking ceremony is continued today in the community of Papunya in the Northern Territory.

Another Arrernte man, Wenten Rubuntja, talks of how the old women used to put emu fat or kangaroo fat into a wooden coolamon, and then use it as modern mothers use baby oil.

When a child was born the women sang the fat and rubbed it onto the baby so that it would grow up strong... If the little one was sung with an emu song then he'd stand up just like a little emu, saying *'Tha tha tha tha'*... We grew up fat and strong after being rubbed with fat. They rubbed all of us with fat so that we would grow up quick. My old grandmother, Laddy Arleye, and old Annie mob, they used to rub the fat onto us, the old women. That was the olden time Law.

Labumore (Elsie Roughsey) was born in 1923 on Mornington Island in the Gulf of Carpentaria. She describes how only the aunties and grandmothers can attend the birth.

Fathers, brothers and grandfathers, too, cannot see the baby or the mother until the child is a month old or more...

After these times, then the babies are allowed to go and visit the father and grandfathers. They are kissed by the whole family, nursed by them and loved by them. Gifts are given to the mother and baby, also to the father of the child. Bush bark baskets are made and presented to the child.

A plant that was used to make babies healthy was called *ngalurrpu*. People use it even today, whenever a baby is born.

When the sun goes down, the mother and grandmother and aunties take the new baby out into the bush. The baby's brothers and sisters and cousins go along, too.

The women dig a hole in the earth and put dry leaves inside. On top they put sticks, and then some *ngalurrpu* leaves. The grandmother or one of the aunties lights the fire to make smoke.

The mother lets the smoke go around her body and her breasts, to make her strong and well. Then she holds the naked baby and gently turns it over in the smoke.

Sometimes the other *pipirri* (children) cry and say, *'Wiya kutjantjaku ngayuku malanypa!'* 'Don't burn that baby!'

The grandmother says, *'Paluru palya, wiya ulanytjaku! Puyungka palyani palya.'* 'Don't worry for that baby. Now it will be healthy and it won't get sick, because of being in that smoke.'

An Arrernte baby sleeps comfortably in a coolamon, Alice Springs (Northern Territory), 1895.

Family relationships

These days, Aboriginal families tend to be big, but in the past it was common for parents to have only a couple of children. This made it easier to share the food if times were tough. A man who had proved himself to be a good provider sometimes had more than one wife, and kids happily acknowledged their second mothers.

As groups of related families frequently travelled and camped together, children had lots of playmates, as well as plenty of older kids and grown-ups to look after them and teach them.

Knowing family was linked with knowing country. Children knew the names of their relatives and ancestors, together with the names of the special places to which they belonged.

During the twentieth century, many hundreds of Aboriginal children were taken from their families and forced to grow up in institutions. The families never forgot them, and in recent years many have been welcomed home. In 2008 the Prime Minister made an apology to these Stolen Generations on behalf of all the people of Australia.

In the traditional way, Aboriginal people have a second system of family relationships, in addition to their biological family. In English this is often called 'skin', but it has nothing to do with actual skin or its colour.

The skin system means that every child is born with extra mothers, fathers, grandparents, aunts, uncles, sisters and brothers. As well, living creatures and pieces of country are linked to the skin groups. Because of the skin system, every person has a place and a role in society. Skin also lays down the law about choosing a marriage partner, so that close relatives don't have children together.

One of the first things that little children learn is their own skin name, and the way in which the people around them fit into the pattern of skin relationships.

In Aboriginal culture today, it is still common for kids to be 'grown up' by members of their extended family. Particular aunties and uncles take on important teaching roles, and children often live with their grandparents or other relatives.

Kukatja Elder Patricia Lee Napangarti tells a *Tjukurrpa* story to explain how the skin system lays down the marriage laws among her people in the Great Sandy Desert.

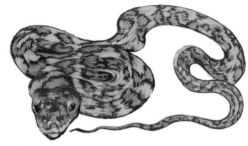

Tjukurrpa story...

That little *taatjaal* [carpet snake] was carrying around lots of people inside its stomach. It was so full up that its stomach opened up like zip and all the people get out slowly, like getting out of the bus. All the skins come out. More and more...

Taatjaal was talking: 'Tjapangarti, you got to marry Nampitjinpa and you got to have Napanangka and Tjapanangka children.

'Tjapanangka, you got to marry Nappurula. You got to have Napangarti and Tjapangarti children.

'Napangarti, you got to marry Tjampitjinpa and you have little Nangala and Tjangala.

'Tjangala, you got to marry Nungurrayi. You got to have Nampitjin and Tjampitjin children.

'Nakamarra, you have to marry Tjapaltjarri and have Tjungurrayi and Nungurrayi children.'

Adding on to Patricia's story, Tjama Freda Napanangka explains how the skin system also applies to every single living creature.

Every one bird – he got skin... and whatever bush tucker – he got skin. Any animal – he got skin. That from Dreamtime, from *Tjukurrpa*. ... Same skin that way, like we.

Any thing, any bush tucker, any animal, any bird... they got skin.

You got skin, you got country!

Across the continent, Aboriginal people have many different Creation stories. Among the Yolngu of East Arnhem Land, the main Creation story is about the two Djangkawu Sisters who arrived by canoe with their brother, and then set off with their sacred digging sticks, creating and naming every single living creature and even the land itself.

In the central panel of this painting by Law Woman Dhuwarrwarr Marika of the Rirratjingu clan, we can see the two sisters giving birth to all the children of all the clans.

This is the sort of story that laid down the Law for how families and skin groups and clans and language groups related to each other. In other places the Creation story might be different, but all the stories emphasise family relationships.

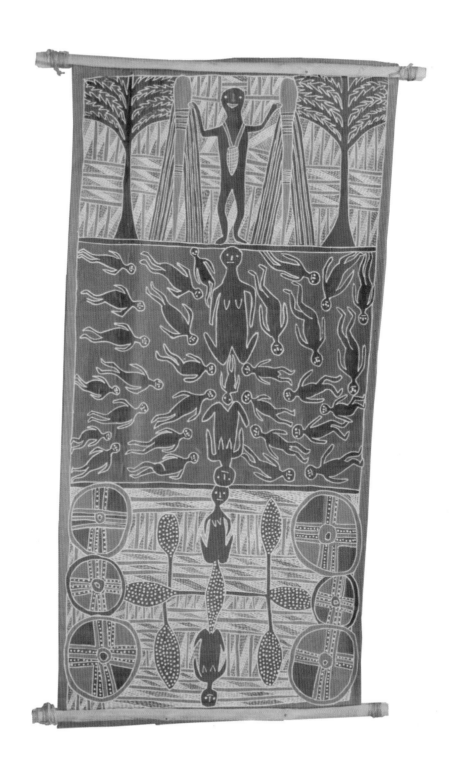

Alice Nannup is from the Pilbara in Western Australia. She describes how the skin system was strictly enforced by the Elders when she was growing up.

Those old ones, they were very strict on the Law, like with the skin groups. There's four to a group – four on the mother's side and four on the father's side. Everyone fits into these and you've got a 'straight', like you can't just marry anyone, you've got to marry straight...

They were very strict laws all right, but it was good Law really because everyone knew where they fitted in and what they could and couldn't do.

The mothers and aunties of a family helped each other to get bush tucker, as shown in the jigsaw below, produced in 1999 as a resource for the Papunya Curriculum. The traditional symbols in the central circle show two women sitting down with their digging sticks and coolamons.

Outsiders often have trouble understanding why the Law allowed men to have more than one wife. Alice Bilari Smith, who grew up in the Pilbara during the 1930s, explains how this practice enabled the women to share the job of getting enough food to feed the children.

Those days we used to be one family all the time. Every family like that. They never say, 'You not belong here.' They used to look after one another all the time...

Good man used to be a good husband, to look after the wife... If he's a good man, look after the wife properly, well he allowed to have three wife. If one wife want to leave him, well she can go. If she want to stay, man looking after her, then she can stay... Wives don't get jealous of one another, they just live together. Used to work different jobs...

Those days it was easy, see, the bush tucker all the time. You nothing to worry about, you don't go buying things from the shop. You got three wives, these wives all go different, different ways, get different, different food, to bring all the food to the camp. And husband going hunting. It's nothing to worry about. You don't spend money, you just go and pick from the tree, or might be in the ground, you digging, or goanna, whatever you kill... Get them kids feed all the time. We never used to be hungry, we used to have plenty food.

Hilda Muir's mother was a Yanyuwa woman from the area around Borroloola in the Northern Territory. Hilda's father was a white man whose identity she never knew. She spent her early childhood as 'a bush child, happy and carefree' with 'a big mob of kids'.

When I lived with my people I spoke the lingo. I was a happy little Aboriginal kid. We just enjoyed life and played, and we were all Yanyuwa. Our mothers all loved us, and our aunties and uncles and nannas too. We were one big loving family, and nobody worried us... The adults never growled at us. They were loving, kind people, our family, I never knew of my people belting their children when I was a child. There was never any belting but there was picking up and holding. Maybe there wasn't much to be naughty about, or too many rules to break.

Then one terrible day in 1928 the eight-year-old girl was taken by police and put into an institution in Darwin. This 'changed [her] life forever'.

I lost my true inheritance, my ancient language and the culture and companionship of my Yanyuwa people. I stopped being an Aboriginal girl and became a half-caste girl. From someone who'd had so much, I was now someone who had nothing, with no past and an unknown future.

Donna Meehan was born in Coonamble (New South Wales) in 1954. For the first few years of her life she grew up happily with her mother, her brothers and sisters and her extended family.

My family were like the local band. My aunts used to harmonise, lots of singing every night around the campfire. We'd have guitars and my mum would play button accordion, or piano accordion. My grandfather would play an old squeezebox, uncle used to play a mouth organ. The other uncle would play a gum leaf. And it was just this beautiful noise... So you'd go to sleep at night with the singing.

When Donna was five, her mother was forced to give her up. Donna vividly remembers the moment of separation on the railway station.

When the train shunted forward, I was scared, and then when I saw my mum and my grandma and my aunt standing there crying, I just didn't understand what had happened... I just remember crying for hours... It's something I've never forgotten and I think because that was the first time in my life I ever knew what fear was.

Adopted by a white couple in Newcastle, Donna grew up as an only child. Many years later, when she made contact with her mother and family, she felt that she didn't fit in.

Seven years after this reunion, Donna's mother died. Finally, at the funeral, Donna felt her own connection with family.

I had an overwhelming sense of belonging. I had been searching for something all my life but didn't know what I was searching for until this moment and now it was so easy to identify. I needed to know what I belonged to. I needed to know I was part of a family and I needed to know I was part of a race. It was much more than needing to know, it was a matter of wanting to belong as well as feeling I belonged. I became one of them and they became my people. I could now say I was Aboriginal knowing it was coming from my heart and not just my head.

On 13 February 2008, the Prime Minister of Australia, Kevin Rudd, said Sorry to the Stolen Generations and their families for the pain that they had suffered as a result of the government policy of removing Aboriginal children from their families. This photo shows some of the many hundreds of people who gathered on the lawn outside Parliament House, Canberra, to hear the Apology made on behalf of all Australians.

The men sitting at the front of the photo with the 'Sorry' sign are two of Donna Meehan's brothers, who were Stolen from Donna's family along with Donna herself and four other siblings. At the moment this photo was taken, Donna was walking towards them. She says, 'There was healing in numerous ways that day.'

Leah Purcell grew up in Murgon, in Queensland, in the 1970s.

You know, some people say 'Have you got a big family?' and I say 'Probably a thousand.' And I probably would, if I did a count. And it goes beyond just blood. The blackfella community is massive and family is important. It might drive you up the wall sometimes, but it's very important. And I love it!

I'm the youngest of seven, and my mother had seven sisters, and they all had five to ten kids each, so it was a massive family – a lot of aunties. And even my mum's cousins became aunties because in blackfella way, they're sister-cousins. So when my mother passed away, they became mothers.

This photo was taken by Axel Poignant in Arnhem Land in 1952. The camp, at a waterhole near the Liverpool River, had been established by a senior Kunibidji man called Mangawila, who had two wives and a growing family. There were three other campsites nearby, and all the families were related. They frequently moved around and camped together.

Mangawila's family were in this place at this particular time to gather palm hearts, which they processed and ate. These families were completely self-sufficient in the bush, and only went to the mission station about once a year, when they had something to trade.

Andrew has grown up in an inner suburb of Sydney, as his father did before him. Though he lives far from his traditional country, Andrew connects with his heritage through the things that his family teaches him.

My dad's dad lives a couple of houses down from us, and when I was younger I'd go and see him every day when I come home from school. He told me stories – Dreamtime stories – and also the history of the family. He taught me to respect people, to respect the Elders, and when I was in about Grade 4 he taught me the didg. I've been playing it ever since.

For Tasmanian Aboriginal people who had been taken from their homelands to the Bass Strait islands, it was particularly important to maintain family links through celebration. At Christmas time, the men on Cape Barren Island used to sneak off and light a line of fires down the hills, to mark Santa's journey for the kids. Gloria Templar remembers this from her childhood during the 1940s.

On Christmas Eve all the children would sit around outside of the houses and sing and play games waiting for the Santa fires to come down the hill. As soon as the fires neared the bottom of the hill, all of the small children would race inside and hang their pillowcases on the mantelpiece around the fireplace and head off to bed. We dared not ask how long it would be before Santa came...

Christmas Day was the best day of the year. The women would start to prepare the feast for lunch early in the morning. All of the children had to be outside playing with their toys while the bigger girls helped in the kitchen...

Lunch was usually locally grown meat and vegetables that were available at the time. The puddings were something special, though. The puddings were usually made on the island and were always shared with family and others who visited on Christmas Day. There were always lots of visitors on Christmas Day. Everyone visited everyone else.

Alice Rigney is a Narangga Kaurna woman who grew up on the Point Pearce Mission (South Australia) during the 1940s. She was the oldest of fifteen children.

When I was growing up on Point Pearce it was a family set-up. Everyone knew everyone else's business and what you were up to. You could never get up to anything that wasn't considered appropriate to the family and the culture – what was deemed the right thing to do and the right way to behave. There were always uncles and aunts looking out for you and looking over your shoulder, so you had to do the right thing. But you wanted to do that anyway because they gave you so much love and support and assistance, so you wanted to do the right thing by them.

Lola James is a Yorta Yorta Elder from Victoria. When she was a child her family lived in Mooroopna, but every weekend they went to the Cummeragunja Mission, to visit relatives and to pay their respects at the graves of Lola's grandparents.

The old Koori tradition of knowing extended genealogies is still going strong. Koori women held this knowledge of kin before the Invasion, and keeping it up since then is very important to our identity as Indigenous people. I keep up the tradition of teaching family history, and my children will do the same with their children. It's necessary to help Stolen Children to find their relations when they return to our communities. It's also important that we know which land we belong to and have to care for, which land we can finally claim native title to.

Homes

For most Australians, home is the centre of life.

For Aboriginal Australians, however, home is much bigger than just a house and garden. In many Aboriginal languages, people use the same word for 'campsite' and for the whole area of country which belongs to their language group. 'Home' means the homeland, and everything in it.

A campsite was like a house: there were different 'rooms' for different purposes and for different family members. The area where food was prepared was kept very clean. Parents and children slept together at the main camp, and they sat together around a big fire at night. Young men had their own campsite, a little distance away, and when boys reached puberty they went to stay at the young men's camp. Girls remained at the family home until they were married.

Towards the end of the nineteenth century and through the first decades of the twentieth century, many families were forcibly moved to missions and government reserves, where they were crowded together in squalid conditions. Residents were not allowed to come and go without permission, or even to receive visits from relatives. They were forbidden to speak their language. And yet for kids who were born and raised there, the reserves and missions became home.

In traditional time, families might stay in one place for weeks or even months, if there was plenty of food and water there. Alternatively, during a journey, a home might just be a place to stop overnight. Over generations, people returned again and again to the same homes, where large or heavy belongings (such as canoes or grinding stones) were left for next time.

Naturally, Aboriginal homes were built in various ways, to suit different types of weather and environment.

All of this began to change with European settlement. As homelands were turned into farms and pastoral properties, the sheep and cattle drank the waterholes dry and ate the grass that had provided grazing for native animals. Unable to get bush tucker, Aboriginal people were increasingly squeezed off their land and into camps on the edges of towns. One survival strategy that people used was to get jobs on pastoral properties, where they set up home in favourite places.

In the 1970s, as the campaign for Land Rights really took off, some groups of Aboriginal people moved back to their country, and established outstations.

These days, most Aboriginal people live in towns and cities. However, they continue to identify themselves by the name of their traditional country and language group. Many continue to fight for the right to control their own housing, while others are still struggling for recognition of their Land Rights.

Bob Randall spent the first seven years of his life with his Yankunytjatjara family on their homeland near Uluru. In 1941 Bob was taken from his family and sent to an institution called 'the Bungalow' at Alice Springs.

When I was a child I lived in a home without walls. The stars were the ceiling of my house and the earth was the floor. The horizon was just the entrance to another bedroom. Nothing separated me from the wind, the heat and the cold, or the sounds of the birds and insects that lived in my country. For seven precious years I lived like this, and through the stories told to me as we walked through country or sat around the fire at night, this landscape and everything in it was my intimate family...

As a child I felt I had total freedom and I could go wherever I wanted at any time. There were always the eyes of so many aunties, uncles, mothers and fathers watching for my safety. Everybody was responsible for each other, that is *kanyini*. In this way the *Tjukurrpa* Law of *kanyini* informed every aspect of my universe.

When I was a young boy it could get just as cold as it does now but we adjusted our body temperatures to keep warm by getting close to other people. On a really cold night we would invite the dogs to sleep with us. If the wind was blowing, the mothers would pick a spot for us to camp that was in a low area among the sand-hills, where the natural movement... of the wind could be directed away from us. If we were on flat country they would make windbreaks out of tree branches and shape them like a horseshoe, and put clumps of grass on top of them to create shadow or a shelter. Everyone in the family would then sleep close together inside this one walled area.

All the elements of nature were part of our life experience. When it rained we got wet and when there was a flood we moved to higher ground. We didn't worry about what happened to us. If a shelter was washed away we built another one when it was needed.

Our actions were always determined by our needs. We didn't plan anything. We had no intention of staying in any one place permanently, so we didn't build permanent shelters. Everything material was very temporary. What was permanent was *Tjukurrpa*.

We were all bound by the Law of *kanyini* from the time of the *Tjukurrpa*, the thread of connectedness, caring and responsibility that links *walytja* (family and kinship), *kurunpa* (spirit and soul in all things) and *ngurra* (my 'country' or home). It was this that I lost when I was taken away, as happened to so many of my people.

Jack Mirritji describes how different campsites in Arnhem Land were designed for different seasons and purposes.

We had a bush shelter called *gurrukurru*. It was a wooden platform hut, built on top of a high post, so that on hot days it would be cool inside. It had a stringybark roof about ten feet above the ground, and there we slept during the dry season. During [that] season we [also] used a shelter called *bumaluga*, which gave us shade...

There was another hut called *gilkal*, which was used for keeping mosquitoes away. This was made out of paperbark stretched over a framework of sticks. It looked like a beehive. It had four big doors, and a smoky fire inside to keep the mosquitoes out during the night.

Sometimes, when I used to go hunting with my father, it would happen that we would stay overnight somewhere away from the camp. But as the ground was wet, we would make a camp in the trees.

We looked for a big tree and made steps in the trunk. Then, where the big branches started, we would make a platform from paperbark and the leaves of the tree, for a sleeping platform. On the outer branches of the tree we would build another, smaller platform, and strengthen it with wet sand. When the sand dried it set hard as cement, and a fire could be lit on it.

The 'born country' of Rita Huggins was the land of the Bidjara-Pitjara people, now known as Carnarvon Gorge, in north Queensland. After describing how 'our people lived in this land since time began', Rita talks about the various homes where she lived as a child in the early 1920s.

This way of life abruptly ended when everyone in the extended family was forcibly removed to Woorabinda. Yet this was not the end of the journey. Within a short time, Rita's family was moved on to the government reserve which would be known as Cherbourg.

The caves were cool places in summer and warm places in winter, and offered shelter when the days were windy or when there was rain. They offered a safe place for women bringing new life into the world. As had happened for my mother and her mother before her, going back generation after generation, I was born in the sanctuary of one of those caves...

We [also] lived in humpies, or gunyahs, that the men built from tree branches, bark and leaves. Gum resin held them together. We would sleep inside the gunyahs, us children arguing for the warm place closest to Mama, a place usually kept for the youngest children...

One winter's night, troopers came riding on horseback through our camp. My father went to see what was happening and my mother stayed with her children to try to stop us from being so frightened...

Dadda and some of the older men were shouting angrily at the officials. We were being taken away from our lands. We didn't know why, nor imagined what place we would be taken to. I saw the distressed look on my parents' faces and knew something was terribly wrong. We never had time to gather up any belongings. Our camp was turned into a scattered mess – the fire embers still burning.

What was to appear next out of the bush took us all by surprise and we nearly turned white with fright... We had never seen a cattle truck before. A strong smell surrounded us as we entered the truck and we saw brown stains on the wooden floor...

It took the whole night across rough dirt tracks to reach our first destination of Woorabinda Aboriginal Settlement. Woori was a dry and dusty place compared to the home we were forced to leave.

Conditions on the Aboriginal Reserve at Lake Tyers in Gippsland (Victoria) were so harsh that in the 1940s and 1950s some families left and built their own community at a place called Jacksons Track. Shacks along the creek were made from bush materials and bits of tin. There was no electricity, sewerage or running water, but the people were able to control their own lives and to see their families.

Russell Mullett's parents went from Lake Tyers to Jacksons Track in 1952. He was born there three years later.

You couldn't have your relatives visit at Lake Tyers without a permit, and most of the time the manager wouldn't give permission. You couldn't leave without permission, and if you worked you only got threepence an hour plus rations. Outside you were entitled to full wages.

We were free at Jacksons Track. Anybody could come and visit. Your relatives could come and stay and the Aboriginal Welfare Officer ... or the Manager of Lake Tyers couldn't hassle us.

During the summer we were always in the creek swimming or chasing wombats or possums, or playing games in the scrub. And after dark we would sit around the fire, and the old people would tell stories about *mrarts* and *doolagahs* and *narguns*. In our imaginations they were something like Big Foot, big hairy men, wild men, and the *narguns* were their wives.

Today, people are in so much of a hurry, but in those days you had all the time in the world and it was enjoyable sitting down and talking to people and listening to stories... I can remember many nights, sitting up until after midnight, listening to the old ones talk.

My childhood was probably the best upbringing that a person could wish for. We were not always happy on Jacksons Track but we were lucky in one respect – there were lots of old people around to keep us in line. They had hard lives, harder than we had, and they protected us from a lot of bad outside influences.

Outside a home at Jacksons Track, Gippsland (Victoria), in around 1959. Russell Mullett is the little boy who is standing third from the right. The tall boy in the middle of the back row is Lionel Rose, who grew up to be a famous boxer.

Isabel Flick's earliest memories are of 'moving about all the time' with her family, to avoid the Welfare. However, when she was about six they settled down to live at what was known as Old Camp on the reserve on the river at Collarenebri in north-west New South Wales.

There was only about six or seven families when we came [to Old Camp] in 1934, each family camped in clusters close together, you know? Then each of the family camps was spread along a high bank of the river, a long way back from the water. A path came from each end of the bank to a big grassy flat about 200 metres wide then down to the edge of the river...

The houses were [all] made in the same way, but everyone could do it a bit different from the others. They'd build a bush timber frame and put flattened tins over it. The tins were kerosene tins or some square tins. You'd fill them with water and put them on the fire. As they boiled, the seams would burst and then you could hammer them out flat. The roofs were tin and some houses had breezeways, the windows were small and the rooms were dark inside. The floors were dirt, but they were swept so much they were smooth and hard. Outside was swept too. And people usually built a bough shade up against the house and we used to live out there a lot of the time – in summer 'specially.

In the 1950s the government established a settlement at Papunya in the Northern Territory. People from five Aboriginal language groups were removed from their lands and brought together in one big camp of over a thousand people, mostly living in humpies made of wood. By the mid 1960s, some people (especially people from the Pintupi land to the west) were moving to outstations, to get away from Papunya.

Linda Anderson Tjonggarda was born in Papunya in 1962. She describes how her family joined this move to the outstations.

People were choosing to go to outstations so they can grow their *pipirri* (children) up. Papunya was too many people, too many people from different languages, different *ngurra* (countries), all mixed up together. And people were homesick to get back to their country. They wanted to be in their family groups – like, we were Pintupi, and we wanted to live with Pintupi.

So when I was about seven my family joined up with five other Pintupi families and we moved to Alumbra. There was a big mob already at the outstation when we got there, maybe three hundred people living there in tents, but it was a good place for families – away from the fighting and the grog at Papunya. A happier, quieter place. People were doing ceremonies, going hunting.

There was a kitchen that was run by Spider Tjampitjinpa and Topsy Napangati. They used to cook lunch for the whole school every day. The kitchen was just outside, open fire, with a bough shelter. Same with the school. We had no building, just a shade area and the blackboard. Terry Parry was the teacher – he lived at Alumbra with us.

At Alumbra there wasn't a store, but a truck came every second Friday from Papunya, and people were buying their food from it. Flour, sugar, tea. And every day when we were at school our mothers and grandmothers were hunting, so after school there would always be fresh food – like *rumiya* (goanna), *akatjirri* (bush sultanas), *malu* (kangaroo) – all fresh.

About a year after we moved to Alumbra, big rains came and flooded the creek, and the truck couldn't get through for some time. Because of the floods, people couldn't go out for bush tucker. Everyone began to complain as we were running out of food. There was only dry damper and tea.

Soon after this, a lot of the people who were staying at Alumbra decided to move to another outstation, called Kakali Bore. (Some people call it Yai Yai.) There was a lot of moving around at this time because people were looking for a good safe place to live. The same families that we'd come with to Alumbra, they were moving to Kakali, and again we went with them – my mother and stepfather, my big sister and my grandmother. My little brother Justin, he was born there.

At Kakali Bore, there was a windmill to pump up the water, and again everyone lived in tents. Terry the schoolteacher moved there with us, and set up a new little school. But when I was about ten, my mother and father must have thought 'Let's go back to a decent school' – maybe because I was growing up. And so we moved back to Papunya.

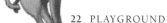

Rininya is fourteen. She spent her early childhood in Sydney, where she is now enrolled at a boarding school. In the holidays she lives with her Wiradjuri mother, grandmother and great-grandmother, and her brother and sister, near the New South Wales Riverland town of Griffith. Rininya talks us through her home, and tells some family history from another mission.

Back home, I live on the Mission. We call it 'Three Ways', 'cause there are three ways to get into it, but they've blocked off one of the roads now, so there's really only two ways to get there. But everybody still calls it 'Three Ways'. Or just 'the Mission'. It takes about an hour to get to town, 'cause we walk real slow. But in a car it's like ten minutes.

There's about fourteen houses at the Mission, and they're built out of bricks. My mum and us, we stay with my nan and my great-nan. She's turning eighty next year, and we have to look after her 'cause she's getting sick, and that's why her son is next door. He's my nan's brother.

My mum told me that my great-great-great-grandmother grew up at Warrangesda. She got *taken* to that mission. When I was younger, my nan and my mother and my great-grandmother took me there for a visit. It was weird and spooky – all old houses falling apart.

This is what Three Ways is like...

When you go out from our house there's a road, and then the irrigation channel and the pipes. You can jump off the pipes and into the channel and have a swim, but there's parts you can't go or the water *takes* you. And you can walk across the pipes into the bush. Sometimes we play hide-and-seek there, or us kids just muck around there.

If you keep going down the other way, there's a dam, and you're not allowed to swim there. If you do, you sink down in the middle and that's it! Mum tells us not to go there.

Another place we're not allowed to go is this house where there's real bad spirits. And sometimes we can't go to the park, 'cause there's magpies, and they swoop you.

The Mission is a good place to live, because at night time, all us kids, we go to the Corner and all hang out there. It's a safe place, because if my mum wants me, she always knows where I am, and she can call out and tell me when it's time to go home and go to bed. Because the Corner's not far from home, and there's a little street light. And Three Ways is safe 'cause all your cousins and family are there. It's a good place to be.

This linocut, made in 2009 by Badger Bates, is called 'Mission Mob and Bend Mob, Wilcannia 1950s'. It shows the Darling River looping around the tight rows of houses that lead up to the mission school.

The artist was raised by his extended family and his grandmother, Granny Moysey, from whom he learned about the language, history and culture of the Darling River.

Mother tongue

All babies start learning language from the very first moment they enter the world. By copying the sounds that they hear spoken around them, they start to communicate in their mother tongue.

At the time when Europeans arrived, there were about 250 languages and perhaps another 250 dialects spoken across the continent of Australia. For Aboriginal people, as for people in other parts of the world, speaking a particular language is part of belonging to a specific homeland. Just as people who live in England speak English, the people who live in Warlpiri country speak Warlpiri. Even if people no longer speak their mother tongue, their language-name is still their way of identifying their connection to an ancestral homeland.

While all children in the traditional way spoke their mother tongue, many kids grew up speaking a number of languages. A child might have a mother who came from one Aboriginal nation, and a father who came from another. And because families travelled across many countries, kids would meet up at ceremony time and learn new vocabulary as they played together.

These Yolngu babies are learning their mother tongue in a loving family.

With the coming of European settlement and the removal of Aboriginal families to missions and government reserves, the speaking of Indigenous languages was discouraged and even forbidden. Mothers were often frightened to pass on their own mother tongue to their children. Over time, many languages stopped being spoken. Yet while some words were kept as secrets, other Aboriginal words – such as 'kangaroo' and 'Canberra' – became part of the general Australian vocabulary.

These days, most Indigenous kids have English as their first language, or they speak a form of Aboriginal English that is sometimes called Kriol.

In remote communities, children still often grow up speaking their traditional language. In some of these places, schoolchildren learn how to read and write in their mother tongue, as well as in English. This way of schooling (called bilingual) is the easiest way for all children to become literate. However, in recent years some governments have insisted that Aboriginal students learn in English only.

In some other communities, where the traditional language is no longer spoken in daily life, Aboriginal people have begun to reclaim their traditional languages and to teach some of the local vocabulary to Indigenous and non-Indigenous children.

In the Northern Territory community of Papunya, five Aboriginal languages are regularly spoken, but the community has chosen Luritja as the common language.

Linda Anderson Tjonggarda, who was born in 1962, gives a wonderful description of how she learned her mother tongue... and how she went on to teach it, both to her own children and to children at Papunya School.

When I was a little *pipirri* and I was ready to get fed, my mother would say, '*Amma... amma*,' and she'd point to her breast, so that helps me to understand what she's saying. '*Ngalyara ammaku*,' she would say in Luritja: 'Come here for milk.' And she used to repeat it for practice: '*Amma*.' And I would say, '*Amma... amma*.' And my mother and my grandmother would clap and praise me. '*Palya lingku!*' ('Very good!') '*Kungka palya!*' ('Good girl!') And as I got little bit bigger she would teach me other words like *ulkaman* (old woman) and *nyuntu* (you). And body parts – *tjina, mara, kata* (foot, hand, head).

But if I crawled up to the fire, she would call out, '*Waru!*' ('Fire!') She would use tone and model it for me, so I would know never to go near the fire again.

And *pilkati* the same. If we saw a snake, or just the track of a snake, she would cry out, '*Pilkati!*' and I would know to be afraid.

So my mother was speaking to me all the time in Luritja, never in English, and I was speaking back to her. *Uwa!* (Yes!)

When I first start hearing English, it is when I am going to the clinic for the nurse. So the first English words I would learn are 'sick', 'guts ache' (for diarrhoea), and 'bandage', 'medicine' and 'needle'.

And then when I start school there's 'pencil', 'paper', 'Sit still!', 'Be quiet!', 'Listen!' – the classroom words. And every time when we used to come into the yard, the teachers used to say, 'None of those languages! No more language!' And if they heard us speaking language they used to say, 'Stop that crap!' *Yilta!* (True!) The teacher and the principal would say: 'I never want to listen to that crap. When you are at school, speak English only!'

After moving to an outstation and then back to Papunya, Linda's family moved to the nearby community of Haasts Bluff when Linda was about thirteen. A Pintupi teacher called Murphy Roberts gave the students great support inside and outside the classroom.

When I went to Haasts Bluff, that was my first bilingual school. Papunya was English only, but at Haasts Bluff we were learning writing in Luritja. We were able to read in two languages, so that gave us more opportunities. Every Saturday was our hunting day and we used to go out from an outstation called Utility. When we'd come back, Murphy would get us to write a little story in language about what we'd got – maybe honey ant, or goanna...

When I had my first daughter, Natasha – at the beginning, when I looked at her eyes, I didn't know what to do, but Mum said, 'Come on, that's your *pipirri*. You're the teacher.' And so I taught her, same way as my mother taught me.

When Natasha was ready to feed, I used to say, '*Amma! Amma!*' And soon she would say, '*Amma, amma*.' And I used to say, '*Tjikila!*' ('Drink!') And she would say, '*Tjikila*,' and she would drink. And when Natasha used to say it properly, I used to clap and say, '*Palya lingku! Kungka palya!*'

So that the things that I was taught by Mum were passed on to my children.

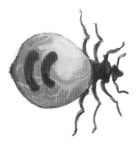

Same way now, teaching the *pipirri* in the [preschool] classroom. I am teaching them how to speak Luritja properly.

In the morning we start off with a song, like the body parts song, and a little bit of free play. Then we come back and have a story in Luritja. In preschool it's still all in Luritja, but now the policy is English only again for the bigger kids. It's like going back to the past. It has really closed the door. *Uwa.*

Donna Daly and Raymond Ingrey are members of the La Perouse Aboriginal community, based on the shores of Botany Bay, where the traditional language is Dharawal.

Like all the people of the Sydney basin, the Dharawal suffered terrible losses in the first wave of Invasion. Those who survived were forbidden to speak their language.

Now, however, the Dharawal language is being revived at Gujaga, the local Aboriginal preschool. In the Gujaga program, the Elders teach the language to the preschool teachers, who in turn teach the children at both Stage 1 (aged 0 to 3) and Stage 2 (aged 4 to 5).

Gujaga's administrator, Donna Daly, grew up on La Perouse Mission in the 1960s. She explains why she learned only English.

When I was growing up, I was never allowed to learn the language. My grandparents wouldn't teach it, they were too frightened in case they'd get in trouble with the government or the Aboriginal Board or whoever.

When I was young, I had both my grandmother and my great-grandmother alive. And they used to speak the language, but not so people could hear them. And if you were to say, 'What was that word?' they would say, 'Hush hush.' And if you were to say to them, 'Can you teach us?' they would say, 'No, we're not allowed.'

I would have loved to have been able to learn the language, but they wouldn't teach you anything because they were in fear of getting in trouble.

Raymond is a generation younger than Donna. He was enrolled at Gujaga preschool when it began, back in the early 1980s. After explaining why language is crucial to culture he describes the Dharawal language program.

My language group is Dharawal, the language spoken in the Botany Bay and Illawarra areas. My grandmother's mother was Dharawal. She was born on La Perouse beach in 1884, and her mother was Dharawal, so that's where that line comes down from.

For any Aboriginal person, who you are and who your mob is – that's what makes you stand proud. That defines who *you* are, as a person. Language connects with everything. You know, it connects you not just with the people you are living with today, but it links you with the old people, and it connects you to your country. It is virtually your spirit, I suppose. And language for an Aboriginal person – well, your language and your land go together. So you know where your land is, you speak that language – there's not much more than that!

For a number of years now, I have been working with the Elders in a co-ordinating role, assisting them to collate all the language research material that they have collected over the years, and helping to develop the language program and some little books to use as resources for it.

In Stage 1, the children are learning to identify their body parts – eyes, ears, nose – and they're responding by touching their nose. At the end of the year, one or two kids will say *'Ngayagangguli nugar'* ('This is my nose'). In the room for older children, they're using language for short sentences – such as *'Waddha njindiganguli dhanba?'* ('Where is your hat?') – and learning words for family – *ngaba* (mother), *babaa* (father) – and for the landscape – *gundhu* (tree), *gurabang* (rock), *djaadjaa* (moon), et cetera.

The issue is that the kids pick it up so quickly that the rate they learn is quicker than the language teachers are learning it! The Elders are well aware of this.

Ricky is from the Gumbaynggirr nation, whose traditional country is the area between Coffs Harbour and Kempsey, on the north coast of New South Wales. He is in Year 9 at a Sydney boarding school.

Where I'm from, the Elders got together and made a language centre, called Muurrbay – it stands for 'Tree of Life'. They've made a dictionary of our language and they're trying to get the language back into the community. They're working in about four schools now, doing language classes with all the students. We're getting it put into the non-Indigenous education system as well.

I know how to speak Gumbaynggirr, but I have to keep learning it. I don't really *have* to do it, but I choose to do it. Back when I was in Year 2 my uncle started coming to primary school and he was teaching the language and I thought: 'Oh, that's good to have people trying to teach us the language again.' So I thought I'd stick with it.

Even here at boarding school, I've got a dictionary up in the dorm and I try to keep up with it. That book was given to me as a gift, because I'm the youngest speaker who can speak the language as good as I do. So they gave it to me late last year at the book launch of the dictionary.

It's a bit hard, learning by myself, and I get tired, too. I actually sit there and read through the book and try to memorise the words and what they mean, and it gets a bit hard sometimes. But I have to keep up with it. Because I got to finish my Aboriginal education as well as my non-Indigenous education. And that's part of it – learning the language.

Born in 1984, Evelyn Dickerson is a Noongar from Perth. She now lives in Sydney with her Koori partner and their son, Mundarra, to whom she is teaching her language. Beeliar was traditionally spoken by the people from the wetlands south of the Swan River.

Even though we were living in the city in Perth, my family still speak language, so I grew up knowing my language. It's called Beeliar. And though I live in Sydney now, I want my son to learn it.

I've just had my little brother over to stay, and he still speaks language, and he was teaching my son. And even though Mundarra doesn't speak at all at the moment, he'll sit there and listen and watch our faces and mouths as we speak in language, and he'll try to say something.

I'm trying to keep it strong with him.

Left: These children at Gujaga Aboriginal preschool at La Perouse are having a Dharawal language lesson. Child-care worker Petra Silva takes the children as a group through the vocabulary for the parts of the body. Petra then calls 'Yumba!' ('Come!') to each child in turn, so that the children have a chance to practise the language individually.

Right: Evelyn Dickerson with her son, Mundarra (aged 20 months), at the Multi-Mix Mob Playgroup, Marrickville, 2009.

First lessons

Aboriginal babies get so much attention from their mothers and aunties and grandmothers that they don't need elaborate toys to distract them. Sometimes, however, in the past, seashells or snailshells were strung together with hair or vine-string to make a rattle, or a big seed pod might be used as a plaything.

When infants were teething, they were given necklaces to chew, made of bark or roots. The bush medicine inside these plants soothed the babies' sore gums.

Wherever they went, the women always took the little ones with them. Often a coolamon or a basket was used like a carry-cot. When babies became toddlers, they were carted around by their big sisters and cousins.

As they tumbled about in the arms of their relatives and older siblings, little children quickly learned essential lessons around the campsite. Naturally, there were strict rules forbidding children from playing in the drinking water, or touching the fire.

At an early age, children also learned which animals and plants could be eaten, and which ones were poisonous or dangerous.

Other early lessons were to do with relationships. As a child came to know her skin name and the skin names of people around her, she learned how to fit everyone into the jigsaw of community and country.

These important social lessons continue today. In some urban areas, Aboriginal communities have established their own preschools so that little children can have their first lessons in a culturally familiar environment.

Opposite page: In this photo taken by Axel Poignant in Arnhem Land in 1952, a mother, Mamerirrnginj, lovingly holds her first child, Djabbiba. The family still live in the community at Maningrida.

Below: These grandmothers at Kakadu are making a turtle out of string to amuse the little ones, 1990s.

Roy Kebisu, from Yam Island in the Torres Strait, was little more than a baby when he was inspired to join the tradition of dance and song which is such a vital part of his community life.

I have memories of lying down on a coconut mat in a dance area here on Yam Island where my aunts and uncles are singing a dance song, and watching all my other aunts and uncles coming in to dance the island dance.

It made me feel good, it made me want to join with them. When I was old enough, anyway, I was eager to join with them. Because seeing them dance when I was small gave me the inspiration.

Morndi Munro was born in about 1909 in the Kimberley. His language group is Unggumi. After describing himself as a 'born in the bush kid', he goes on to talk about the first lessons he learned.

I was carried around in my coolamon, just a lying-down boy. Then I moved from there and came out from my coolamon to sit by the fire, sitting and lying on my belly on the ground. I only knew drinking *nunyas*, milk from a breast. I was getting bigger now, I didn't want to stop with my mother all the time. I started to walk outside, away from the fire.

When I was a growing boy, my mother took me around with her before I went with my father. I learned about getting sugarbag and where to find it. We followed up that sugarbag bee to its nest in the tree. She would climb right up and I would watch her, learning, getting my experience. That's the first thing my mother showed me.

And my mother took me around to eat yams, that's bush potato. We call it *inyanayi*. I used to sit next to her with my digging stick and dig in the ground. At first she would mash up the yam and I started to like food. When my mother thought that I had learned to pick up all the yams for myself, she told me, 'Now you can get tucker and you can feed yourself.'

In the Kimberley area, mothers and grandmothers help little children learn the first important layers of the Law in the practice known as *wuduu*, as Daisy Utemorrah explains.

The children had their lessons every day. Early morning and in the evening their grandmother and their mother warmed their hands and touched [the child's] forehead, eyes, nose, mouth, hands, and right down to their feet, which meant *wuduu*, the warming of hands. When they touched the forehead, that meant to give; and the nose, not to go around to another person's fire; eyes, not to see evil things, and not to love up with strangers; mouth, not to use bad language; hands, not to steal what doesn't belong to you; and the feet, not to trespass on other people's land.

Bronwyn Penrith grew up in the Tumut area in the 1950s. As well as being a mother and grandmother, she is Chair of Mudgin-Gal, an Aboriginal women's centre in Redfern. Bronwyn explains how the important lesson of sharing is passed on to little children.

We are people who come from a culture of sharing, so there's not really a lot about the singular person, about the individual. Traditionally, we've lived for each other, sharing everything, and we still live like that today, with that sense of community.

When I try to think how this is passed on to children, the first thing that springs to my mind is the sleeping arrangements. For as far back as I can remember, I always slept with someone. And those were the occasions when the stories were told. You'd get in close to Mum or Nan to hear the stories. Even though you heard them every night of the week, you still wanted to hear those stories.

And I think today – certainly in *my* home – when my daughters come home, and the kids, we put all the mattresses on the floor and then the women and kids sleep together. Turn the TV off and start yarning. And the kids ask for the stories.

So I think the first part of sharing is that you always share your person, yourself – your space. And from that goes everything else. You share your food and your clothing – everything else!

The right way of learning

Traditionally, Aboriginal children learn within the extended family. Uncles and aunties as well as parents and grandparents do the teaching. Older kids also pass on knowledge to the younger ones, especially in the playground of the bush.

Although there is a lot of freedom, there are strict rules about the right way to do things. Children are expected to watch and listen, and then copy what their teachers are doing. Asking questions is seen as ignorant or even rude. Once the method of doing something has been observed, children are expected to practise over and over again, until they get it right.

Above all, the Aboriginal way of learning is collaborative rather than competitive. Children work together to succeed as a group, rather than trying to be the quickest or the best as individuals.

In recent years, Elders in various parts of Australia have set up special classes or even their own schools, in order to pass on knowledge and culture by the traditional method. This is often described as 'two-way learning' because it combines Indigenous and non-Indigenous education.

Yankunytjatjara man Yami Lester grew up in a traditional way during the 1940s. He describes how learning was included in every moment of a child's life.

When you travelled along with your fathers or mothers they'd be teaching you, telling you which type of food you could eat and which was for the animals; the names of the plants... They'd show the bad tucker to you and you'd learn not to touch it; it's only for the kangaroos and other animals. The mothers taught the girls in the same way about food; where to look for honey ants and how to dig for them ... or it might be to do with grass seeds. The women have special stories for this food, and the men have stories to do with hunting emus and kangaroos. The kids learn like that. They'll tell stories not only to do with the land, but also stories about how people should behave...

You must learn to do things correctly; you can't do them wrong. Other people can see if you aren't doing things in the right way and if you aren't, there will be trouble for you or a member of your family as a result. We'd be frightened of that.

Walmajarri Elder Jukuna Mona Chaguna describes how she learned the skills she would need when she became a wife and mother.

When I was a child, I was taught to use a coolamon for separating seed from the sand and bits of grass. My grandmother took my hands and held them under the coolamon. 'This is the way you separate the seed,' she said as she showed me how to shake it. She taught me not to jerk the coolamon around, because then the seeds wouldn't separate properly. I didn't really master that separating action till a long time later, when I was bigger. By then I could do a good job of separating the seed from the debris.

In the past, there were no books or computers to store information. People had to remember everything they needed to know for their survival.

Hazel Brown, from the southern part of Western Australia, talks about the role of the Elders in passing on knowledge.

From our old people we learned the rules. We were taught the rules, the traditions of Noongar people and the rules and laws of our old people. Everything was explained to us; we didn't have to go and read about it in someone else's book. What we knew, we learned it from our old people.

This Pitjantjatjara man is teaching these boys how to make a spear. In his left hand he holds a woomera.

Andy Tjilari describes how he learned to make a spear when he was growing up during the 1930s in his traditional Pitjantjatjara country. His father's spear-thrower (or woomera) had a sharp stone attached to one end, so that this multi-purpose tool could be used like a chisel.

As a child I learned from my father. This is the way he taught me. He broke off a tecoma branch and put it in the fire and when it was hot he flexed and straightened it while I watched. I thought to myself, 'Ah, it's straight now.'

Then he scraped off the bark and when it was straight, sharpened it again with a spear-thrower. This is how I learned, watching continually as my father worked, thinking to myself, 'Ah. So that's how my father makes it.'

Next he broke a branch from a mulga tree, cut and sharpened it. After sharpening it he notched it and joined it to the spear. After making it level he tied it with kangaroo sinew.

As he tied it, I watched and learned, and I asked my father, 'Father, what is this you are doing?' He replied, 'No, you must watch and learn.'

As a boy I did not observe very closely what my mother did – only a little. The girls would watch her and learn about native millet. Mother collected the seeds and put them in a wooden dish and then she took a small rock and ground them.

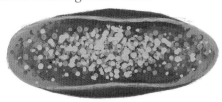

Evelyn Crawford was a Paakantji woman, from western New South Wales. These memories are from the 1930s, when she was a young girl living with her family at Yantabulla.

The white man's school was only a part of our life, and not the most important part. We had the whitefella school all day, then in the afternoon we'd have to learn all our Aboriginal training. Our teachers were our grandparents and our oldest aunty – in our customs she's our second mother... But the most special teachers were uncles – our mum's brothers, not Dad's...

There were eleven of us in our mob, mainly Paakantji kids, all related. There were other classes too, different tribes – Muruwari, Wangkumarra, Burunji and Ngemba. Their languages are different, but closely related. All tribal kids could speak Burunji... but when you got older, say thirteen, fifteen, you had to talk the language of your [own] tribe...

A kid started in the class as soon as he could talk. Even small kids had to learn to walk long distances without shoes because that was part of the traditional way of life...

The Elders believed that to be really skilled at anything you had to devote all your time and interest to it. We all learned the basics in all parts of Aboriginal learning, so that we knew enough to make a sensible choice. Then we 'specialised' in the thing we were best at, or were really interested in.

On the Furneaux Islands off the coast of Tasmania, the right way of making shell necklaces was traditionally passed down from grandmothers and mothers to daughters. There were two stages of learning. Little girls had fun helping to collect the right shells from the beach, but it was not until they became young women that they learned how to string the necklaces. Today, mothers are still passing on the knowledge to daughters. Three women who grew up on Cape Barren Island in the 1940s share their memories.

Gloria Templar begins.

Most of our weekends we would go with my grandmother. She was a shell necklace maker and we used to go with her to gather the shells from the beach. We'd walk for two or three hours before we'd even reach the beach, and we'd put the day in there then. She'd be looking for shells, gathering shells, and we'd be getting the shellfish and eating them, and saving some to bring home.

We would sit up there on the beach and just play around as children – we'd have to wait till she was ready to come home. Sometimes it would be dark before we'd get home.

Gloria's cousin Muriel Maynard joins in. She used to go out collecting with Gloria and their grandmother.

The women used to have special ways of cleaning the shells, too. [As little girls] we was never allowed to do it. They'd use salts, and put the shells in to bring the meat out, especially the maireeners – they had to be cleaned.

Gloria remembers something else.

One thing we had to do to help, we had to walk in the water, pick the shells off the kelp. We'd help do that. And shake the kelp so the shells would fall off.

Our grandmother would show us: 'This is where you look to get such and such a shell.' And that's something we've always remembered from those days, so we've been able to go back and look in the spots for those shells. I think if you didn't know where to look, you'd probably never find them.

Lola Greeno collecting shells with her daughter Vanessa on the east coast of Tasmania, 2002.

Lola Greeno talks about passing on the tradition in the twenty-first century.

Even though my daughter Vanessa lives in Christchurch, New Zealand, she comes home once or twice a year, and the time before last we went shell-collecting around lots of different beaches around Tasmania, and she made some bracelets. We went collecting during the day, and we sat down sorting and washing and cleaning the shells, and *making* at night. And this time she was home, she made a long necklace. She's very proud of it...

I've got a grand daughter – she's only a baby at the moment, but I'd like this [tradition] to be handed down to her. Vanessa is absolutely totally engrossed in this and I know for sure that she will carry it through the family. I've even said to her, 'If something happens to me, I want you to make sure that the grand daughter gets to learn how to do it.'

Wandjuk Marika was born in 1927 in his traditional country in East Arnhem Land. He was a member of the Rirratjingu clan of the Dhuwa moiety. On page 13 there is a picture of the Djangkawu story, painted by one of Wandjuk's sisters.

I was born on a little island called Dhambaliya
which is Bremer Island.
I grew up in the bush
and learn all about what my father taught me
and my mother taught me.
My mother was for cooking food
and my father was for hunting,
and at the same time he took me to the bush and was
    teaching me about the creation, land creation,
about the animals and the food, what to eat, what not
    to eat,
what to get, which is the right food,
which is the wrong food – that we are not allowed to eat,
which is the very important special food
which is only for Elders,
not for the young people.

Also he taught me about the land,
    who owned the land, what part of the different tribe
owned the land,
and also he taught me things about my tribe or my religion,
where they came from, where their land is, how we are
divided up into Dhuwa and Yirritja.
He told me about the many way and teach me.

I learn about the song,
I learn about the dancing,
the special dance and sacred song and sacred implements.

I was been grow in the bush to be well and fit
And he taught me about where to go, how to live, what
    to find.

When I became about fifteen years of age he taught me
how to hunt for turtle –
go out in the sea, see which turtle right one to kill,
and I was taught how to use the turtle spear, turtle rope
    and harpoon.
I learned where is the good place to hunt the turtle for
    battling in the sea.
Also most important,
he taught me about the Wawilak and Djangkawu creation
    story.
I learn where to go,
what part of the country my own people own,
which part other people own the land,
like Gumatj, Manggalili, Djambarrpuyngu, Madarrpa, Djapu,
    Galpu, Naymil and all the others...

My father was taught by my grandfather and his father was
taught by his great-grandfathers coming for years, story for
centuries and centuries, generation to generation.

Now I *know*,
I know *right* now,
where to go, what to find, how to teach,
how to paint, what the story I am doing.
This is my life story and I can go through the bush
    by myself,
so I can find more courage, more power.

Sheridan has grown up in a family of six brothers and one sister. She is from the Biripi language group, and her home is near Taree on the mid north coast of New South Wales.

My uncle, he's an Elder of Taree, and he can tell you these things from when he was growing up, and it's like he passes a lot of knowledge on from when he was growing up. Sometimes he might take us on walks, and show us sacred sites, and it's like you're kind of being connected to the land. And he talks about the responsibility of looking after those sites, and passing on the knowledge to younger generations. Like, where we go camping every Christmas at Saltwater and Wallabi – that's the main place where most of the sacred areas are shown to us by my uncle.

It's kind of a tradition for the family, like a get-together. There's two beaches, with two surfs and a lagoon, and we take tents and set up camp in the middle, in between the beaches. Go swimming, fishing, snorkelling... relax and have fun.

And my uncle, he's a really good storyteller. Sometimes at night time he sits us kids down in his campsite and tells us all sorts of stories – ghost stories, and family stories. And he tells us how we are related. Being older, I listen, and find out the information, whereas my younger brothers don't worry about it as much.

Tiwi writer and educator Magdalene Kerinaiua is showing the big book she has written in her traditional language to children on Bathurst Island (Northern Territory), 1988.

When Linda Burney was a little girl, she loved playing school, so it is no surprise that teaching was her first career choice. However, teachers also need to learn. Here Linda describes how she learned from her Aboriginal students and their parents, and how she used Aboriginal practice in her classroom.

I became actively involved in Aboriginal affairs when I was a schoolteacher in Mount Druitt in 1979, and I got to know a couple of the parents who were part of the local Aboriginal Education Consultative Group (AECG). And that's when I got involved.

My real teachers were particular women and a number of men that I came into contact with through the New South Wales AECG. It was a community-based organisation and I had the good sense to understand that part of Aboriginality is listening and watching. And I learned in this way from very senior people who were involved with the AECG.

I was also fortunate to have the opportunity to work in the very early days of the Aboriginal Education Unit of the New South Wales Education Department, and this took me out to many Aboriginal communities around the state. And I was told very early, 'Don't think you know everything, because you don't. A piece of paper doesn't mean you know everything.' That made sense to me. And I had some wonderful shoulders to lean on.

In my own classroom I decided that 'These kids are going to love learning.' That's what I worked on, for children to love learning, to feel that – no matter what their skill-level was – everyone got a chance.

The most important thing I had in my classroom was the notion of sharing – this is an Aboriginal thing – and we'd share down to the point where we'd sit in a big circle in my classroom at lunchtime for the first ten minutes, and everyone had a sandwich whether they brought their lunch or not. The room really was a complete sharing environment where children weren't judged, and I don't think I remember any bullying – it was a really lovely atmosphere.

I have always said that there are many things in Aboriginal culture that it would serve the broader community well to adopt. And you know – observation, demonstration, and the collaborative *sharing* approach that goes with Aboriginal learning – I think that's fantastic teaching practice, and it works with children.

The traditional way of learning through going bush with family continues today. In the photo below, Thanakupi (Thancoupie Gloria Fletcher), from western Cape York, draws in the sand as part of an explanation to her two young grandsons. Also with her in the picture are her sister, cousin and nephew.

Journeying

Over a large part of Australia, the soil and seasons aren't suited to the kind of intensive agriculture that is practised in Europe. As well, Australian marsupials such as the possum and the kangaroo can't be domesticated and used as farm animals in the way that European people have used mammals such as the sheep and the horse.

Over many thousands of years, Australia's First People developed a clever way of dealing with these circumstances. Instead of staying in one place and becoming farmers, they moved about according to the seasons and harvested food when it was plentiful. Instead of burdening themselves with lots of material possessions, they travelled light, and treated the land as their home.

In order to live like this, people needed to know their country off by heart. From the moment they could walk and talk, children started to learn to read the signs of the seasons, and to memorise the landmarks. They needed to know the best way to get from one place to another, and where to find water and food on the way. Otherwise they might get lost, or even die.

Learning country was like learning a story, because every hill or waterhole had a name that linked it to the actions of the ancestors, who were seen as creating the land by their journeys. Travelling to these Dreaming sites and performing the right ceremonies was a religious obligation.

When Europeans came, Aboriginal people were pushed off their land. Many families went on the road in the hope of keeping out of the way of the authorities who wanted to move them to reserves, or put their children into institutions.

This journeying enabled people to continue to make their pilgrimages to their sacred sites. Although traditional ceremonies were banned in many areas by missionaries and government officials, Aboriginal people were quick to find new reasons for huge gatherings. Even the missionaries couldn't forbid families from celebrating Christmas!

These days, sporting competitions and cultural festivals are often the reason for journeying. As well, people travel long distances for Sorry Business.

A big mob gathered to celebrate Christmas at Jacksons Track, Gippsland (Victoria), in around the early 1950s.

For the Aboriginal people of the Furneaux Islands, journeying was done by sailing boat. Molly Mallett, who grew up during the 1920s and 1930s in the small settlement known as The Corner on Cape Barren Island, describes the family visits that she 'really loved' most.

Once a year we would travel to Badger Island and spend a fortnight with my uncle and aunt and their five daughters and one son. We would leave The Corner about nine o'clock in the morning – that's if the tide was right. In those days, it was a wooden sailing boat, no motors – we had to depend on a bit of wind to fill the sails. It used to be a slow journey at times. The men would put the couta lines out with a bit of white cloth material on the hooks – caught many a couta that way. The boat would be anchored and we would be rowed ashore in a dinghy. We would arrive with our bags over our shoulders and head for the cookhouse. We knew there was a meal waiting for us – which would be cold wild turkey and vegetables, then [we] filled up on scones and cream.

In the 1930s Depression, Hazel Brown's family in the southern part of Western Australia worked and camped on various farms in their traditional country. They also went on the road.

If work was scarce at the farm, well then mostly we travelled around and we'd be hunting. We had two kangaroo dogs, and we'd go around to different waterholes and stay at different places; sometimes it might be a government dam on the side of a road, or sometimes a waterhole.

We used to go camping out there, stay for about a week. Till they shoot all the kangaroos out, and then light a fire behind, like to burn all the scrub where they hunting, and then shift further down to another waterhole.

That's how we came to be familiar with the bush, and Dad'd show us middens and old camping places where they used to go and hide from the police when they were kids, old campsites and places where something happened that was significant to them.

Margaret Tucker was born in 1904 at Hay near the Murrumbidgee River, and grew up in the two communities of Moonahculla (near Deniliquin) and Cummeragunja. Her father was Wiradjuri, and her mother's people were from Cummeragunja.

I remember going walkabout as a child. White people would call it a holiday. However, a walkabout was a useful holiday. My people did not go walkabout at random. They went to pastures that were not new to them. They knew when these pastures would be flourishing with fresh growth...

On hunting trips, I remember being carried on my old aunt's back in a possum rug, warm and snug, the gentle rhythm rocking me to sleep...

Walkabouts were a source of wonder and delight to the children. Tiny as we were, we would take part in wading through swamps, chasing bandicoots and young ducks... Possums when caught for food would often have a young one, which we would rear and keep as a pet. They were lovable things.

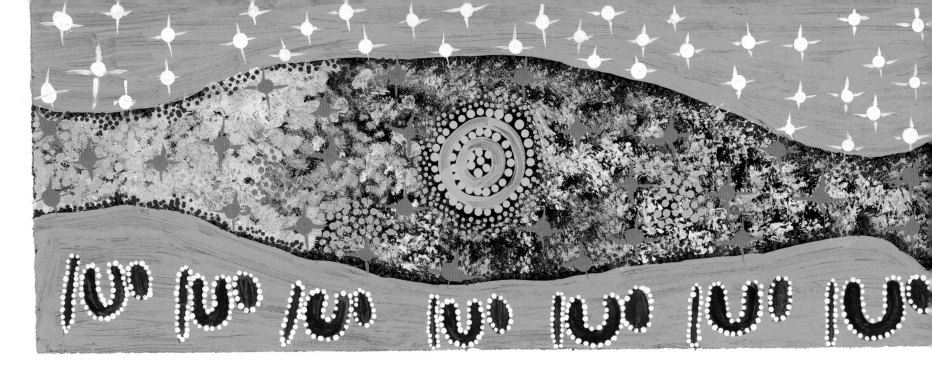

Wiradjuri woman Shirley Smith grew up during the 1920s at Erambie Mission, near Cowra (New South Wales). One of her earliest memories was of going on a journey with her grandparents to Grenfell, where her parents were working as drovers.

The wagonette rolled on. Peeping from the canvas flaps in the back, I could see the green hills rolling past us. We seemed to have followed an almost straight line, leaving the line only to find a smoother or more shallow place to cross a creek or empty water course. My grandfather always liked to travel in a straight line. He stayed away from the white folks' roads and railway lines, for he said to follow them was the fastest way to end up lost.

With the sun almost high in the sky we rested. Grandfather would take the horses out of the harness and let them rest too,

under the shade of a tree where they would nibble at the cool green grass. Grandfather liked best to stop beside running water and we would cool down by putting our feet in the water and splashing it over our arms and faces.

We would eat the food which Grandmother Emma Sion prepared and then lie down and wait for the heat of the day to pass. Grandfather always used to say, 'Get up with the sun, eat with the morning, and travel with the freshness of the day...'

[After the midday rest] we all climbed back in the wagonette and travelled through the fading afternoon. Just before last light we would stop and Grandfather would again unhitch the horses and make an evening camp for us.

The night sky was very important to Aboriginal travellers. It was both a calendar and a navigational aid. It was also a picture book, full of stories about celestial journeys. This painting by Papunya artist Punata Stockman depicts the story of the Seven Sisters, who can be seen sitting with their digging sticks and coolamons beside the Milky Way.

Hopie Manakgu is from the community of Gunbalunya, situated in Kakadu National Park (Northern Territory).

I remember my childhood days as being free and homely because the bush around me made me feel I was its own. There was no barrier or restriction, it was as if it was intended for me – and it was.

I spent most of my childhood roaming with my family, travelling on foot and by canoe collecting food like fish, goanna, wild honey, turtle, wild berries, lily roots and kangaroo.

Deanna McGowan was born in 1962 in the Pilbara region of Western Australia. Her maternal grandfather worked as a government dogger – trapping the dingoes which menaced pastoral stations. During school holidays he often took his wife and grandchildren on working trips, which would last for up to two weeks at a time.

Going bush was the happiest times for me in my childhood.

My grandfather was provided with a Land Rover... We would pack our swags, clothing and tucker box and be squashed in the back of this small vehicle.

We would live off the land, only ever taking flour, tea, sugar, salt and pepper. Off we would go, in all kinds of conditions, very hot (no air-conditioning), dusty, squashed, and to places where there were hardly any roads.

During the day, our grandfather would drop us off at a nice river, where we would spend our days fishing, swimming, playing or being taught by our grandmother the ways of the bush. Our grandfather would return in the afternoons [to] collect us... Once we found flat ground, we would set up camp, which involved rolling out our swags, and we would help our grandmother prepare the evening meal. Afterwards, we would lie in our swags side by side, staring up at the stars, as our grandfather told us all kinds of stories about our culture, his life and the land.

Ngarrindjeri/Nganguruku woman Jenny Giles grew up during the 1950s. Like many Aboriginal people, her parents lived in fear that their children might be taken away. They survived by trapping native water rats and selling their skins. These rats are much larger than common rats, and in the 1950s their beautiful fur was used to make luxury goods.

I grew up on the Murray River near Nildottie. My father was a fisherman during the open season on Murray cod, and the rest of the year we'd spend travelling by boat between Renmark and Wellington trapping water rats for a living.

My parents always feared the Welfare coming and finding us living in an old shack so I think that was one of the reasons that we kept moving. We had a little boat and we'd load it up with all of our stores, like flour and things...

We'd just travel around, maybe row about seven miles, maybe camp where there was a big swamp or something, where we thought it was going to be good for rats. I think Dad had about 120 traps and they would have been the most valuable possessions that we had. That was how we made money – we couldn't get money from anywhere else.

If there was one place we thought was trapped out, we'd move along a bit further, maybe another seven miles and camp again. We'd stay in wurlies, even in the winter time... At night we'd just all roll in together and go to sleep.

Galarrwuy Yunupingu grew up in north-east Arnhem Land in the 1950s. As he travelled about, hunting and gathering food with his family, he learned to read the seasonal calendar of his Gumatj clan country.

Moving camps was something that Aboriginal people culturally had for the purpose of learning – not only catching and living off the land for health reasons, you know – it was at the same time teaching children. Going through the country and teaching children the names of the places and all that. I've treasured that, you know.

You start sitting in the one place and you raise the child, and you're stuck in the white man's style, white man's type of schooling, and you just read the maps and all that. It doesn't relate to a child.

Whereas to us in our day we moved on, we touched the soil, we saw it, we experienced it – you know, where the billabongs were, where the rivers were, where the hills were, what the name of it [was]. We were told in the process, you know, as we walked through. We plucked the foods from the trees and learned the names of the trees as we ate... There's a lot more to a flower than what you see, you know. You can interpret... whether it's time to collect seagull eggs or time to collect possum, [or if] a certain fish is running. You know, everything relates.

Getting water

Across Australia, getting water is the first key to survival. For the people of many different Aboriginal nations, the most important spiritual being was the Rainbow Serpent, whose twisting journey through the land had created the water courses. He was also responsible for bringing the rain that gave life to the plants and animals.

Whether they set up their home for a few weeks, or just stopped for a night, Aboriginal people always liked to camp near fresh water. If there wasn't a creek or a waterhole, people might dig a soak, or collect water from trees.

From an early age, children learned how to find water for themselves, even in the hardest circumstances. They also learned not to pollute the drinking water by playing in it.

Charlotte Phillipus grew up in the 1950s in the settlement at Papunya, to the west of Alice Springs, but her family continued to live a very traditional life.

When we were little *pipirri* (children) we would see the mothers and aunties digging with a stick in the sand, and then we'd see the *kapi* (water) coming into the little hole, and we'd know that was the way to find it. And if we were going near the *karru* (creek bed) and we'd see birds flying around and around, we'd know there would be water lying there.

And maybe our grandmother would show us where to find the waterholes when we were out in the country, and we would have to remember and go straight to those waterholes next time. And when we went out and stayed in the *ngurra* (country) for hunting, Grandma used to tell us *pipirri* a story at night, a story about *kapi* from the people who have been living there first, the people from the *Tjukurrpa*. And the story might tell us where the water travels, and where the water stops. Our grandmother might tell us a story for water and she might do it as a drawing on the ground – showing us where to get water, and we'd have to find it.

These Papunya children are digging for water in a dry creek bed during a school science excursion, 1999. The river red gum growing nearby shows there is water underground.

This river in western Cape York (Queensland) cuts a snake-like track through the land.

Jack Mirritji from Arnhem Land talks about various water sources that he learned about during his childhood. It was impossible to travel far on the floodplain in the wet season, so it was during the dry time that people made journeys and visits.

In the dry season we walked to the inland away from the coast. All the waterholes and billabongs were dry and people from the islands like Milingimbi, who were visiting relatives in the inland, were dying for water, but we and other hill country people knew how to get water from the paperbark tree.

These trees stand near the billabongs or swamps. When we cut the flat part of the tree all countrymen can drink the water juice coming out of the tree. It is salty water, not very delicious, but when you are dying for water you are glad to drink it. In Jinang we call it *maraka*, paperbark-water.

When we were camping near a beach, river or dried-out billabong during the dry season we knew another way of getting water... by making a hole with a digging stick near these places. It takes a long time to dig a hole deep enough for the water, and the first water will be dirty. But after a while it will become cleaner and it is all right for drinking. However, it still tastes strong.

In the wet season there is plenty of water and you can drink water at every place.

Lola Young was born in 1942 in the Pilbara area of Western Australia, and was taught in the traditional way by her Yinawangka grandfather. She passes on a special code of behaviour for those who go to a permanent waterhole.

You have to respect the *yinta*. A *yinta* is a special place where the water never dries up.

The *palkunyji* (python) lives in the *yinta* pool. If you find a *palkunyji* at the pool, do not hurt it. It belongs there and holds the water. If you hurt the *palkunyji* the *yinta* pool will dry up.

If you have never been there before you have to greet the water. You put a little water from the pool in your mouth and blow it so it sprays, then say *ngaarta nhurrara*. It means, 'I belong here'. The *palkunyji* in the pool will smell you and taste you as the water falls back into the pool. The next time you come back he will know who you are.

Getting bush tucker

Kids always have fun getting bush tucker. There's time to explore and play as the work is going on, and there are delicious things to be eaten on the job.

Traditionally, it was the women who were responsible for getting a great deal of the food that kept the family alive. Seed for bread, fruit and vegetables and berries, eggs and insects: all of this bush tucker was gathered by the mothers and the aunties. Often, girls and young boys helped. While they were learning, little girls had special miniature coolamons or dilly bags to store their food in, and some had their very own digging sticks.

Although babies and toddlers went on expeditions from the moment they were born, the littlies were not expected to do difficult or tedious work. During the hot part of the afternoon, children usually stayed with the grandmothers back at camp, where they played or listened to stories.

As the mothers and aunties harvested the food, they passed on their knowledge about the plants and the animals and the seasons, so that when girls grew up they would be able to get food for their own families.

From a very young age, children also learned the important lessons of sharing food and water with each other, and not being greedy. These lessons were reinforced by Dreaming stories in which terrible things happened to selfish people who broke the law of conservation.

In some places, people were forbidden to eat the animal or plant that was their totem. As well as helping to preserve the various species, this law was a way of reminding everyone that human beings are related to the natural world.

When people were forced to give up their traditional lands and go and live on missions and stations and government reserves, they were given rations of European food – mainly flour, sugar and tea. This diet lacked the vitamins that are in bush tucker, and people always tried to supplement their rations with food that grew wild around the mission.

Today, many Elders are still taking children out bush and teaching them how to get food. And whether people live in the country or in the city, sharing continues to be an important part of Aboriginal life.

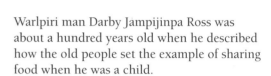

Warlpiri man Darby Jampijinpa Ross was about a hundred years old when he described how the old people set the example of sharing food when he was a child.

All the old people were digging for bush potato. They used to dig for bush potato and would give it to others, or share it among themselves. All the old people would share their food. Oh, they were the good old days we were living!

The old men would go hunting for meat. They would kill *mala* (rufous hare-wallabies) and *pakuru* (golden bandicoots). Aboriginal people would hunt and kill them for food. They would share the food with other families. It was really good in those days when we used to share. We would give meat, and other people would give water – trading or exchanging for food...

The women would dig for bush potatoes and they would pile them up. They would give the young bush potatoes to the smaller children. All our parents would give us bush tucker.

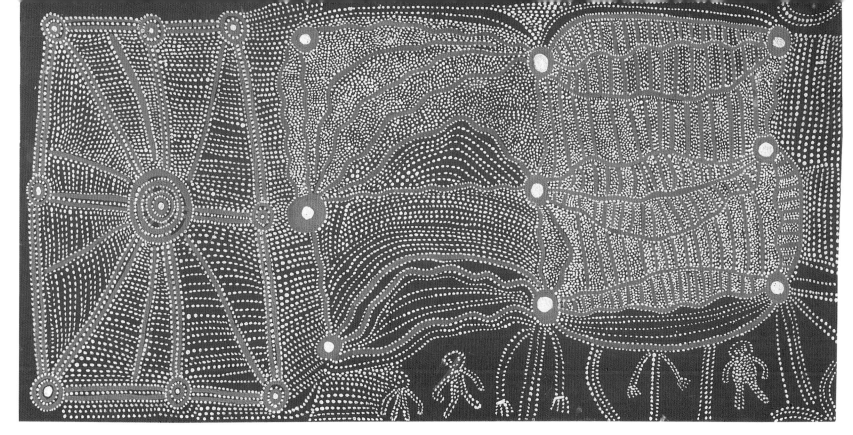

The painting 'Naughty Boys' Dreaming' by Pintupi Elder Mick Namerari Tjapaltjarri tells the story of three greedy boys who ate all the sap lollies growing on the mulga trees around a big waterhole. They were punished by the Two Old Men because they broke the laws of sharing and conservation. (The men's heads are hidden in the picture because their ceremonial headdresses should not be seen by children.)

Conservation was one of the lessons taught to Hazel Brown and her brother Lenny, who grew up in the southern part of Western Australia.

One thing Daddy always taught us, if we found a mallee hen's nest – me and Lenny would have known just about every mallee hen's nest in the Jerramungup district, that's how mad we used to be for mallee hens' eggs – Daddy always said you mustn't take all the eggs. Not like *karder* – racehorse goanna, you know – you can take every one. But *ngaw* – mallee hen – we always left one egg there for the mother. We never ever killed a mother mallee hen.

And if the eggs had chickens in it you weren't allowed to touch them. You were only allowed to take the fresh eggs.

Diane Phillips is a Gunditjmara woman from south-west Victoria. Her mother grew up at Lake Condah Mission, which Diane often visited as a child. Here she tells her mother's story.

Mum had a tough childhood. There was often not enough to eat ... All the Koori families at the mission would hunt for bush tucker to keep themselves alive, 'cause if you relied on the rations they gave us, well you just starved. We got kangaroo, rabbits, eels, whatever – and we'd share it with the other families. Kooris always do that – we had to stick together to survive back then, but we've always shared because that's one of our traditions and we still do it today.

Margaret Tucker describes getting wild dandelion greens (*buckabunge*), and a type of yam (*cumbungie*) as she moved about with family in the area between their homes in Moonahculla and Cummeragunja.

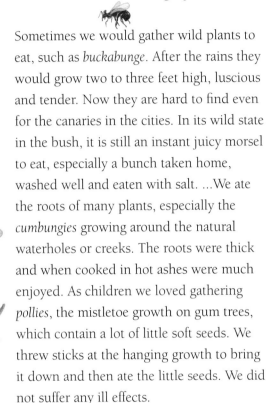

Sometimes we would gather wild plants to eat, such as *buckabunge*. After the rains they would grow two to three feet high, luscious and tender. Now they are hard to find even for the canaries in the cities. In its wild state in the bush, it is still an instant juicy morsel to eat, especially a bunch taken home, washed well and eaten with salt. ...We ate the roots of many plants, especially the *cumbungies* growing around the natural waterholes or creeks. The roots were thick and when cooked in hot ashes were much enjoyed. As children we loved gathering *pollies*, the mistletoe growth on gum trees, which contain a lot of little soft seeds. We threw sticks at the hanging growth to bring it down and then ate the little seeds. We did not suffer any ill effects.

I don't know where the little bits of sweet-tasting substance like honey came from that we found in light bark an inch or two long or on dry gum leaves. We called it manna, a Biblical name. It was a sweet, as good as lollies.

Mary Malbunka painted this picture of the sugarbag expedition. The uncle has a steel axe. A couple of decades earlier, people used stone axes for this kind of job.

Mary Malbunka remembers an occasion on which she and her family went out into the country around the Northern Territory settlement of Papunya to get *ngalypuru* (bush honey or sugarbag).

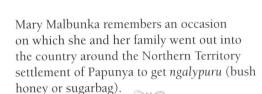

As the ute went along the track, through the *tjaṯa* (bush), we kids were all looking out to try to see some *ngalypuru*.

After a while, Uncle Long Jack called out, '*Nyawa!*' 'Look!' He was pointing towards a tree that we call *arrkinki*. 'Look at the little bees going into the tree. Maybe there's sugarbag inside.'

Now that we knew where to look, we could see the bees against the blue sky. They are small black ones, and they don't sting you.

The moment the ute stopped, we all jumped out. '*Ngalyara mantjilaka ngalypuru.*' 'Come on,' we shouted. 'Let's get that sugarbag.'

Uncle Long Jack had an axe, and he started cutting into the tree. '*Watiyakutu ilala tjampita,*' our uncle said. '*Ngalypuru intipayingka mantangka.*' 'Hold the tin up to the tree, so you catch the sugarbag when it starts running out. Hold it close so the sugarbag doesn't fall on the ground.'

Some of us started to scrape out the *ngalypuru* with long sticks. Others held the tin up near the hole in the tree. We dipped our fingers into the sugarbag, then licked them, we were in such a hurry to taste that sweet bush honey.

When Yami Lester was growing up in the Central Desert in the 1940s, people were beginning to use European implements. For example, a broken mudguard might provide a handy coolamon. People were also hunting new wild food, such as rabbits. However, the old lifestyle was still going strong.

Just about every day the women would leave the camp and go for rabbits, *maku* (witchetty grubs), honey ants, all that. Taking digging sticks and *wira* (bowls) made out of wood or maybe an old car's mudguard, billycans, and us kids. Just walking. No camels or horses or motor-car. Out in the bush they would collect different kinds of grass seeds like *wangunu*. They used to take that and make little cakes. They put honey ants with it. Beautiful, beautiful. *Wangunu* and honey ants.

...And then there was *tjuntala* and *watarka* (colony wattle and umbrella bush). We got that too, just down from the camp. Us kids used to help them collect it; put it in the *wira* for the *kungka tjuta* (all the women). They'd say, 'This is good food. He'll come good when we cook it later on. Come on, give us a hand.' So we used to pick them. We used to play and pick it at the same time. And we were quicker than they were. Then they would take them back to camp and cook them in the hot earth. And we'd eat it.

...We had flour, tea and sugar too. You know, rations. But we were eating *mai*, vegetable food we got from the bush... There was always [bush] tucker. No worries, we were never short. The women would teach us about the country and the food.

This woman and child are getting *maku* (witchetty grubs) in the country near Uluru. Although the picture was taken as recently as the 1990s, a wooden coolamon is being used. Little kids love witchetty grubs because the flesh is as soft and sweet as cream cheese.

Läklak Marika and Bunthami (1) Yunupingu are Yolngu Elders from Yirrkala on the coast of Arnhem Land. They still get bush tucker, and pass on their wisdom to the children.

We are the ones who grow up the children here, going out gathering bush foods, feeding [the children] with everything the island provides. We go out in the morning and stay out all day. Gathering is women's job. We take the children, boys and girls. When boys at seven to eight begin to make spears, they stay behind at the camp, begin to distance themselves from the women. When the boys are ten or eleven, then they go with the men for learning...

While we are gathering *dhan'pala* (mud mussels), we are teaching the young ones the right food to collect, what season to collect, educating about the wild fruits, looking at seasons for foods by looking at plants. 'See that plant, that tells us we got good honey season coming up.'

Nature [is] telling stories and we're connected to these natural stories. We don't write it down and give it to the kids; we teach through talking, telling and showing. That's Yolngu way.

Dhuwandjika Marika and her grand daughter Ulpanda gather waterlilies from a paperbark swamp near Yirrkala.
The waterlily stems are good bush tucker, and so are the seeds. The plant is also a symbol of the morning star.

Born in 1942, Betty Lockyer spent the first five years of her life on the Beagle Bay Mission (Western Australia). Under the strict control of the missionaries, people were not free to come and go. However, they still managed to go bush on weekends. Getting tucker was a way for the old people to pass on the culture.

Sometimes we'd go into the bush to look for fruit, honey or other bush tucker. The old women taught us what fruit and plants to eat, the poisonous ones and the medicinal ones. They'd tell us stories along the way, true ones and legends of the area, each either funny or sad. Most of all they taught us survival skills. I was too young to fully understand all this, but I remember the older girls listened intently.

Now that I am older and wiser I often reflect on the past. The things that our grannies were telling us began long ago, before they themselves existed. That was the way customs and traditions were handed down. They had no pen and paper to record things, so everything was kept alive by the people passing on their history and beliefs to their children...

We'd go back to the [mission] colony laden with bush tucker and have a good feed, sharing with the others. No matter who had the most food or caught the most fish or meat, we'd always get a taste of it, even if only a morsel.

By the 1960s, when Ian Abdulla and his family were living at Gerard Mission on the Murray River, the government had taken over the church missions, but the system was still restrictive. For Ian Abdulla, as for Betty Lockyer, weekends were a time when families went bush to share food and culture.

Working at Gerard Mission as a teenage boy, when the government had control over the mission, I used to go out hunting on a Sunday with my aunty and uncle.

We used to go to the swamps to hunt for swan eggs. The nests were sometimes in the open or in among the reeds, and when we did find the nest we would test the eggs to see which ones to eat by putting the eggs in the water... the ones that didn't float were good ones for eating.

We would get a fire going and put on the coals a big tin or pot to boil some of the eggs to eat before going home. The rest were taken home for supper and to share around with the rest of the family.

Getting tucker still provides a good reason to go bush with family. Troy and Geoffrey come from the town of Walgett in north-west New South Wales. They sometimes go out to get emu eggs, which are eaten scrambled, or are carved as art to sell. Here they describe how to get the eggs.

We go out with our family, we just go out with a bucket or a crate, and we look for the eggs. The way we find the eggs – if we go along a road, we might see one emu. And if there's only one, there's got to be another one somewhere, sitting on the nest. So then we stop, get out of the car, and we make noises to try to make the other emu get up. Sometimes they chase you! You got to pick up a stick, or duck down in the bushes. Wherever that other one gets up, that's where the nest is. You got to be careful, go step by step, not to tread on the eggs.

Mostly you find the nest in bushy places, but on some occasions they might be on dirt patches. The eggs on dirt patches are most likely hatching, so you don't take them. Just leave them till next time, let them grow up and they'll have more eggs. But the ones that aren't hatching, you take all of them. Might be eight or nine in the nest. If you take some, the emu won't come back, it'll leave them. So you might as well take them all.

Going hunting

Hunting was serious business in traditional society, but Aboriginal kids had a lot of fun as they learned how to do it.

Getting big animals such as kangaroos and emus was done by fathers and uncles and young men. Children did not go out with them, and nor did women. However, mothers and children hunted smaller animals, such as lizards and possums. The chase was always exciting, and there was usually something good to eat afterwards.

At a very early age, children learned to observe animal footprints and other signs, so that they would be able to track their food. They also needed to know how to recognise and follow the footprints of other people, in case they got left behind in a journey and had to catch up.

In the day time, as the mothers and aunties took the children out into the bush, they would teach them to recognise the tracks of the goanna, the kangaroo, the rock wallaby, the emu or the echidna. Children also learned to read signs such as broken twigs and scratches on a rock, as well as the distinctive droppings that the different animals left.

Girls and boys developed their hunting skills by having throwing competitions with stones and sticks. Kids also loved to throw boomerangs.

A popular spear game was to make a disc out of bark and roll it along the ground. Then kids used to aim their toy spears at it. It took hours of patient practice to learn how to hit a moving target. After Europeans came, tin lids or hubcaps were used as targets.

When blown-out tyres began to appear beside bush roads, children quickly worked out how to use the rubber from the inner tubes to turn a forked stick into a shanghai. Watch out, bird!

From the time when they started to walk, little boys began to play at hunting with toy spears, which they made out of sticks and reeds. Sometimes their fathers made special miniature spears for them.

When a boy was old enough he would be taken hunting by an older family member, so that he could start to learn the job. He would be expected to keep very quiet and watch very carefully.

Fathers and uncles took a strong role in teaching tracking. At night around the campfire, an uncle might draw animal tracks on the sandy ground, and all the children would have turns guessing which animal was represented.

As the traditional hunting grounds were turned into sheep and cattle stations, the grasslands were depleted, and Aboriginal people had to travel further and further to get their meat. These days, men and older boys go hunting in motor vehicles, and they use guns instead of spears. However, women and younger children still use the age-old technology of sticks and stones. People still love to go hunting.

When Douglas Abbott was growing up, his traditional Arrernte land had become a cattle station. However he has happy memories of 'childhood days roaming around with other kids'.

We used to play with little spears that we used to make from tea-tree. We used to make a spear, proper way, burn it like them traditional ways, put it through the fire and straighten it up. We'd walk around with maybe six little spears and we'd go 'hunting'. We'd look for paddymelon [small wallaby] and think that was a kangaroo or something and we'd sneak up.

Pitjantjatjara man Andy Tjilari grew up in the 1930s. He describes how he and his friend Ilyatjari used to practise spearing a moving target when he was growing up at Ernabella (South Australia) in the late 1930s.

There was a big bloodwood tree there and we two kids ran towards it saying, 'Let's play at spearing pretend kangaroos.' We prised off a piece of bark and made a disc... Then Ilyatjari stood at a distance and I threw [the disc] hard so that it spun away across the ground and he speared it. Then he threw it towards me and I speared it. This is how we learned how to spear.

In about 1920 Morndi Munro, from the Kimberley, learned to hunt, and then to share out the meat when it had been cooked.

When I was a bit bigger, my father took me with him learning to hunt. He would spot a kangaroo and tell me to stop... 'You see that kangaroo, watch that kangaroo.' He left me where that kangaroo couldn't smell me. 'Don't move,' he said. I stood up quiet and still and I watched that kangaroo while my father would sneak up with a spear and get close. He waited until that kangaroo stooped down and then he ran up there and put a spear in it. It took off with that spear in its body and we followed [the] blood trail along. It got into the grass country and my father handed me one of his spears. 'Grab that woomera and grab this spear and you sneak up on that kangaroo and try to spear him while he has a first spear from me. See if you can do it.' That's what he told me.

I sneaked up to that kangaroo and put a spear through him. Then my father knocked him with a stick to kill him.

...Next morning, we shared him with all the people... While I was watching all this I knew I would have to do it again myself, so I would hang on to that idea. I didn't want to starve other people and eat my own. I wanted to do what my father did, so I followed that along and I didn't make a mistake.

This photo, taken in the late 1970s in Arnhem Land, shows a young man and two boys hunting with traditional spears. The country has recently been burned, so it is easy for them to see their prey.

Oodgeroo Noonuccal grew up on Stradbroke Island, across the water from Brisbane, during the 1920s.

My father worked for the government, as a ganger of an Aboriginal workforce which helped to build roads, load and unload the supply ships, and carry out all the menial tasks around the island. For this work he received a small wage and rations to feed his seven children... We hated the white man's rations – besides, they were so meagre that even a bandicoot would have had difficulty in existing on them. They used to include meat, rice, sago, tapioca, and on special occasions, such as the Queen's Birthday festival, one plum pudding.

Of course we never depended on the rations to keep ourselves alive. Dad taught us how to catch our food Aboriginal-style, using discarded materials from the white man's rubbish dumps. We each had our own slingshots to bring down the blueys and greenies – the parrots and lorikeets that haunted the flowering gums. And he showed us how to make bandicoot traps: a wooden box, a bit of wire, a lever on top and a bit of burnt toast were all that was needed. Bandicoots cannot resist burnt toast. We would set our traps at dusk, and always next day there was a trapped bandicoot to take home to Mother to roast.

Dad also showed us how to flatten a square piece of tin and sharpen it. This was very valuable for slicing through the shallow waters; many a mullet met its doom from the accurate aim of one of my brothers wielding the sharpened tin. Dad made long iron crab hooks, too, and we each had a hand fishing line of our own.

One rule Dad told us we must strictly obey. When we went hunting we must understand that our weapons were to be used only for the gathering of food. We must never use them for the sake of killing. This is in fact one of the strictest laws of the Aborigine, and no excuse is accepted for abusing it.

These two kids from Papunya (Northern Territory) have just caught a goanna on a school science excursion to the country around the community, 1999.

Aboriginal culture adapts to changing circumstances. When Eileen Alberts was growing up in south-west Victoria, she was taught to use a gun, even though she was a girl. However, in other ways traditional practice was followed.

Girls as well as boys were taught to hunt for food. Ferreting, setting traps, learning how to use a rifle or gun, fishing, making nets, threading worms, slashing, cleaning and skinning whatever we caught. And then we were taught how to cook it.

We were taught to respect all things that we caught and only to take what we needed. We were taught to take care of all the equipment. Girls were taught to skin and clean a sheep. The only animals girls could not touch was the emu and black cockatoo.

Paakantji woman Evelyn Crawford describes how her mother's brother taught tracking skills to the eleven kids in her 'mob'.

Uncle Arch would say: 'We're trackin' birds today. Keep real quiet.'

When we cut a fresh bird track we'd listen, all quiet, to see if we could hear that little bird close by. Sometimes we'd catch the bird and actually make the track with his foot so we could identify it always. Like policemen fingerprintin', I suppose. A big bird would sink into the sand and the pattern of his track would disappear, just a little hollow left, but the tracks of little birds would be distinct on the surface...

When we found a feather, Uncle would ask us, 'Who do ya think lost this feather?' The little kids'd be so happy if they found a black feather and be able to say 'Crow' and be right. We'd carry home all the things we found and keep them in a special place. We'd look at 'em, and talk about 'em, so nobody could forget 'em...

We'd find a goanna's track. Uncle Archie would ask us, 'What track's that?' He'd be testin' us.

'Goanna track.'

'You sure it's goanna and not blue-tongue lizard?'

'No, he's goanna all right. Lizard walks different, his feet turn a little bit backwards, like echidna.'

A goanna track was always exciting because you knew that at the end of the track was something good to eat.

For Yami Lester and his cousins, too, it was the uncle who taught tracking skills.

My uncle showed us how to track. In one game he'd tell us to put our heads down and not look while he walked around softly, and then came to a standstill. We had to try and find his track and the way he went, to where he was standing. He'd say, 'You know where I'm standing. Can you pick which way I walked to get here?' We'd try and pick the way, but we'd often miss.

The others would say, 'Oh, he went this way. He put one foot on this rock, then onto the stick and the grass.'

We'd be able to tell by the grass, because if you put your foot on it you sort of squash the grass, and that's how you're supposed to pick it. And my uncle would say in Yankunytjatjara: 'Very good.'

Kukatja Elder Tjama Freda Napanangka making snake tracks and footprints – a hunting story, 1997.

Mary Malbunka's uncle, Long Jack Phillipus, taught the children tracking during bush trips from Papunya (Northern Territory).

When it was too dark to run around and play, he used to draw in the sand to teach us the *tjina* (tracks) of lots of different animals.

He would say: '*Ngaatja tjina rumiya.*' 'This track is goanna.' Or he would say, '*Ngaatja tjina ngintaka.*' 'This track is perentie.'...

Sometimes he would draw a track in the sand and ask us, '*Ngaatja tjina? Tjina kutjupa? Tjungu tjina ngaatja?*' 'What's this track? Is it different from this other one? Or is it the same?'...

Uwa, that was how our uncle taught us tracking, so that we would be able to go hunting and get our own *kuka* (meat), when we were older.

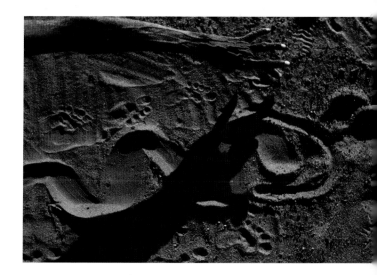

These boys at the Bungalow in Alice Springs are having a spear-throwing competition, 1950s.

As a young girl growing up in the Great Sandy Desert (Western Australia) in the 1950s, Walmajarri woman Jukuna Mona Chaguna learned to hunt her own food.

When I was a child I learned to hunt small lizards to eat. I killed the thorny devil, dragon lizards and small marsupials. I cooked them myself and ate them. Sometimes my grandmother or older sister would kill a blue-tongued lizard for me.

After being Stolen from his Yankunytjatjara family in 1941, Bob Randall was taken to an institution called 'the Bungalow', in Arrernte country near Alice Springs. Here traditional hunting skills came in handy.

When I finally realised that the life of freedom I'd had in the desert was over, I tried to make the best of things. I made friends with some of the other kids and that made it easier for me to accept my new situation. There was a group of us who became very close, and these relationships became a replacement for the families we had lost...

One of our biggest problems at the Bungalow was that we were constantly hungry. The Arrernte kids taught us where to find the local bush tucker, and we made bark boomerangs so we could catch the small birds that came to drink at the waterhole. There were lots of all different kinds of birds then, and it was quite easy to get plenty to eat by throwing our boomerangs among them. When we caught some, we would build a fire and cook them on the spot in the way that our mothers had taught us.

We also supplemented our limited diet with *maku* (witchetty grubs), sugar from the gum tree leaves, pigweed and caterpillars.

Olive Jackson was born in 1930. Her ancestry is from both the Yorta Yorta people of Victoria and the Wiradjuri of western New South Wales. When Ollie's mother died, her Wiradjuri grandmother took in Ollie and her brother Artie and cousin Jim Boy, and 'took to travelling' around the Riverland 'as a way to keep us safe from being kidnapped' by the welfare authorities. Ollie's grandmother got jobs wherever she could – often as a cook for shearers – but the family also ate bush food.

We had a horse and cart and we camped out, sleeping in a tent and cooking over a fire. We'd make damper, and Jim Boy would shoot rabbits and kangaroos. We'd trap possums by putting flour up the bark of a tree trunk and the possum would come along, licking the flour up. We'd hide rabbit traps in the dirt at the bottom of the tree, and in the morning we'd have two or three big fat possums. Possum has a strong eucalyptus taste. Sometimes we'd cook it under the ashes, and sometimes steam it by wrapping it in wet brown paper and cooking it under clean ashes. You have to use the right bark from the box eucalyptus – you can't cook well with dirty ashes. We never ate koala, but we ate goanna, again cooked under the ashes. We also cooked turtle this way, but turtle is really better cooked in a stove.

Ronnie Mason grew up on the New South Wales south coast in the 1950s. For a few years he and his family lived at Nerrigundah, in a tin and bark hut which his father built when he was working at the local sawmill. Other Aboriginal families, such as the Mongta family, lived nearby. European animals were part of the traditional hunting life, whether as helpers (dogs) or prey (rabbits).

At Nerrigundah we ate kangaroos, rabbits, echidnas, fish, beans and other greens. My father taught me how to catch possums. Ten to fifteen young blokes with older ones would go out hunting. We would poke eels out of the river from under logs, poke the spear in and chase them out. When the goanna climbed up the trees, some of the big blokes, like my brother Sonny or one of the Mongta boys, would spear the goanna out of the tree. We'd be down the bottom waiting with the dogs to catch the goanna when he dropped. We had good hunting dogs, beagle hounds and greyhounds. The beagles would chase the rabbits out of the blackberries, out of the holes, and the greyhounds would bring them back live.

In the 1950s Hope Ebsworth and his family lived at Wanaaring in north-west New South Wales. When Hope speaks of 'our country' he means his father's traditional Wangkumarra land, on the Queensland border.

When I was a young fella, Dad brought us out for quite a few trips into our country, and around Wanaaring. He showed us what we could eat out here and what we couldn't eat out on the land. I have taught my girls that. Now I am going to teach my grandkids the same things. We had a good upbringing. We were brought up eating kangaroo, emu and porcupine. We shot these with a gun. Sometimes Dad and us would just camp out and cook the game on the spot.

I remember Dad taught us how to call up an emu by whistling or getting behind a bush and hitting the ground and throwing dust in the air. The emu is very curious. They would come up very close to us so we could get him to eat. Dad used to cook the emus whole in a hole, under the ground, like the old people used to do, and covered them with ashes and dirt.

...Back in those days, even though we were surrounded by the white folks' cattle and sheep, we couldn't afford to eat mutton and beef. We only had it now and then. Otherwise there was only ever our traditional food – like kangaroo, emu, and crayfish and fish out of the rivers and creeks.

Going fishing

Where does the land end and the water start? For Aboriginal people, the sea and the rivers and the lakes and lagoons are part of the country, part of the homeland.

Just as land plants and land animals are spiritually connected with people through the Law, all types of fish and shellfish are also part of the Dreaming. And so are the other sea creatures such as the whales and the dugong, the turtles and the sea birds.

Fishing, like hunting and gathering, was traditionally about everyone working together and sharing the harvest. Even tiny children could help to dig pipis or bait-worms out of the sand.

Families cooked and shared the fish as it was caught each day. At certain seasons, when the catch was huge, hundreds of people gathered for feasting and ceremony.

In the twenty-first century, fish is the most common type of traditional food that Aboriginal people continue to get. Going fishing is also an important family activity, with people of all ages joining in.

Just as children love to get bush tucker or go hunting, they also have fun going out for fish or shellfish. There is always the chance to have a swim, or just to muck about in the shallows.

In traditional time, fish and shellfish were a major source of protein in the diet. For coastal people, the sea and the saltwater estuaries provided a rich and easy harvest for thousands of years.

For generation after generation of inland people, the linking river systems that fan across the continent provided pathways for journeys, with fresh water and food guaranteed.

Harpoons and spears, nets and traps, hooks and lines: Aboriginal people traditionally used a variety of fishing methods, according to where they lived and what they were trying to catch. The materials might have changed but many of these same tools are still being used today.

As for kids getting yabbies: there is no technology that can beat a piece of string and bit of old meat and some sort of net.

On fishing expeditions, children learn on the job as they listen to the grown-ups talking. Coastal kids pick up information about the tides and the weather, and inland children are shown the fishing spots where their grandparents went when *they* were growing up.

Most importantly, kids learn to sit patiently and quietly as they wait for the fish to bite.

Growing up on Mornington Island in the 1920s, Goobalathaldin learned the right way to get the different foods available in his saltwater home. As with hunting on land, there were different roles for men and women and children, but sometimes everybody worked and ate and had fun together.

My mother, older brothers and other relatives made sure that I learned how to do my share of hunting. There is no place in a hunting camp for lazy people. Most of our food came from the sea and was caught by the men. The women gathered shellfish such as oysters and mussels...

We younger boys usually hunted on our own. Every morning we would get up and sit about the fire warming ourselves and talking about where we would go to hunt. If there was any food left from yesterday we would eat that and not go out till later, or when our stomachs told us it was time to go. Being sea people, our lives were ruled by the sea and its tides. With only one tide a day [in the Gulf of Carpentaria] we had to change from day hunting to night hunting and back as the tides changed.

Learning to spear fish, Arnhem Land (Northern Territory), 1991. This boy's spear-shaft has been shortened, to suit his arms, but the prongs are full size. Boys often practise spearing targets of floating bark, until they are able to graduate to small fish.

If the tide was low in the morning we might decide to go hunting the big mud crabs hiding in the mangroves, or go to the areas of exposed rocks on the outer reefs to get oysters, or take our spears and woomeras to get fish, stingrays or turtles in the shallow water.

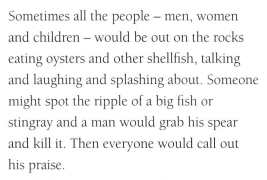

The big fat black-lip oysters are much liked. We used *murrawa* stones and *jilgi* sticks to open oysters and put the meat in small bark dishes. The *murrawa* stones are about as big as a goose egg and trimmed to a point at one end to smash the hinge of the oyster. The shell is then flicked open with the sharp lancewood *jilgi* stick...

Sometimes all the people – men, women and children – would be out on the rocks eating oysters and other shellfish, talking and laughing and splashing about. Someone might spot the ripple of a big fish or stingray and a man would grab his spear and kill it. Then everyone would call out his praise.

We had no regular meal times; everyone ate bits of food they were collecting. Fish would be cooked on the beach soon after being caught and some of it would be eaten straight away while the rest would be wrapped up in paperbark to be taken back to camp for the children and old people, or shared among those who had been unlucky.

Vivienne Mason, from the south coast of New South Wales, is Chair of the Wagonga Local Aboriginal Land Council. In recent years she has been campaigning to have fishing rights recognised by government. She describes the role that fishing plays in teaching culture.

Six generations of our family have camped at Brou Lake. This is a traditional fishing place and teaching ground, to teach young kids about bush plants, medicine, fire safety, cooking, boating. Key survival skills, training and storytelling about our old people. Teaching kids about the environment and to respect the land... We teach kids how to look after the bush, make sure they take the rubbish away. We have access to wild resources for cultural purposes and we were all reared on abalones, periwinkles and pipis.

Lewis Cook is a Bundjalung man from the north coast of New South Wales, where the fishermen traditionally worked in partnership with dolphins. In return for herding fish down the river, these helpers were rewarded with a share of the catch.

My uncle used to wake me up at twelve or one o'clock. The moon would be in and [it would be] low tide, before the change of tide coming in. We'd go down to the point of the island and sit in the middle of the river and we'd wait for the dolphins. We knew they was coming up. They'd come up and we'd go across and get in front of them. They'd just follow along two or three metres behind the boat. We'd row along the river bank, the fish would be jumping in the boat, jumping there and everywhere.

On Stradbroke Island in the 1920s, Oodgeroo Noonuccal and her family used to catch a great variety of seafood, ranging from huge dugong to the delicious crabs which she describes here. As with other forms of hunting, she was taught to conserve the food supply.

Our boat with its chugging two-cylinder engine would finally bring us to our destination, the place where the mud crabs lurked. We had been through the crabbing drill so many times that there was never any need for Dad to give us orders. As we three girls stepped out of the boat onto the mud flats, my younger sister would sieze one bran bag and throw another to me, while my older sister took up the crab hook, which we needed for the crabs that had to be winkled out from beneath the roots of the mangrove trees.

Dad would stay on the boat and follow after us as we worked the flats. He would never permit us to bring aboard a ginny – a female crab. If we did, he would make us take it back again. We would gather enough crabs to feed the tribe, and no more, and we only went crab gathering about once every three months.

In the estuaries of many rivers, the mud flats around the mangrove trees provide a rich harvest of crabs and shellfish. The shallow water of the estuary is also a safe place for kids to practise getting food.

Hilda Muir loved to go bush with her Yanyuwa relatives around Borroloola in the 1920s, before she was Stolen from her family and taken to an institution in Darwin.

Sometimes I hunted with my relatives and Jessie, my sister... We roamed up to Bing Bong and Batten Point and back down to Robinson River...

At other times my people travelled down to the coast for sea turtle and dugong. When they caught fish, turtle, turtle eggs or dugong there was food for everyone – enough to feed everyone in the camp. No one was mean or greedy because sharing is a strong tradition with my people.

Vanderlin Island was one of my favourite places. Out there where we went in season for food and ceremonies, there were little soldier crabs and we used to chase them – not for eating, just for fun. And we climbed the lovely big mangroves.

When the tide was out we would get in the mud to look for big cockles. You could see the top of them sort of sticking through the mud and you'd scoop them and put them on the hot coals, or boil them in a billycan. This is how I spent my time. I travelled with my mother and relatives, going bush hunting to get food from the island and along the coast.

This contemporary bark painting by Marrnyula Mununggurr from Yirrkala (Northern Territory) shows a variety of ways of catching fish. The artist herself says:
'This painting is about traditional ways of hunting – how Yolngu get food from the sea.
'The men are using *lunggu* (harpoon) ready for the turtle and dugong, they go out into the sea with a canoe. Other people are going fishing with a *gara* (spear) to look for *maranydjalk* (stingray). The two people are getting sand crab for bait to catch *guya* (fish) from the rocky places.'
Marrnyula adds, 'We are all connected to the sea through stories and hunting for food.'

Sandy Atkinson grew up during the 1930s on Cummeragunja Mission, on the banks of the Murray River. He often tells young people the story of old man Murray cod, which he himself used to hear on summer evenings when he was a child.

Irene Jimmy grew up during the 1980s with her Gurindji family in the community of Kalkaringi on the Victoria River in the Northern Territory. She was eleven years old when she gave this knowledgeable description of the right bait to use for different fish.

This photograph, taken in 1989, shows Irene Jimmy and some family members heading towards a favourite fishing spot.

After the wet the river falls but there is still plenty of water for several months. Then, during the dry season, the river slowly dries up until only the deepest waterholes are left. These waterholes usually have water right through the dry, so we visit them often to fish and swim... As the river dries up, the fish are trapped in these waterholes so it is easy to catch them. We spend a lot of time fishing for black and silver bream, catfish, pike and barramundi.

Sometimes my family goes out with a big mob of people to a waterhole for the whole day. We buy fishing lines at the store... When we get to the river we look for bait. We turn over stones in the shallow parts of the river looking for freshwater shrimps and small catfish. We hunt for grasshoppers in the long grass and find beetle grubs in the branches of trees. We hunt for frogs in the sand along the river bank...

Black bream, silver bream and catfish like beetle grubs, grasshopper or meat cut up into small pieces. Barramundi like frogs.

It would be so hot and the whole mission might just go down and sit on the banks of the river. Maybe it was starting to cool down. Usually at that time this old man Murray cod would come up and he'd start playing up and down the river and he must have been so big that when he swam along, just a bit under the surface, he created a spout that ran up and looked like a whale blowing up water. In fact, we used to call him a whale. But sometimes in the late evenings, you know, when it became dark, you'd hear him talking or singing down there with his grunts and making lots of noise, and that was him. And my dad tells the story that ... one time, some of the old men decided that they might catch him and so they put their nets in and the next morning when they sailed their boat to get him, he was in the net, he was there swimming around in their net and they pulled him up and as they got up nearly to get him to lift him into the boat he went berserk and he nearly tipped 'em out into the river and he ripped their net to pieces and he got away, and so that became a rule that nobody ever tried to catch him again.

Nicole spent her childhood in the New South Wales town of Walgett. Now Nicole goes to a Sydney boarding school and her mum is based in Tamworth, but in the holidays they go back to Walgett, and go fishing. Nicole's story and map show the way in which fishing is a family social activity that links the generations.

Whenever we go to Walgett, we always go fishing at Mum's fishing hole. There's normally my mum, my aunty Robyn and my aunty Denella.

It doesn't matter whether we catch anything – we just go for the fun of it. And my aunty Denella, 'cause she's the eldest out of my mum's siblings, she always tells me stories. Like about when they were little and stuff, or about when they used to go fishing with my nan in the same spot where *we* fish.

We set up like a little campsite on the bank. I have my line set up near the campsite, and my mum and my aunties spread out along the riverbank. If it's me and my mum and my aunties – just us – we'll cook the fish on the riverbank, but if we have younger kids, like little cousins, we'll go home to cook it.

And sometimes, if the fish aren't biting, then we go looking for porkeypines – echidnas – and if we find them, we take a rock or something to hit them with, and we take them back to the little campsite on the river, and we cook them up.

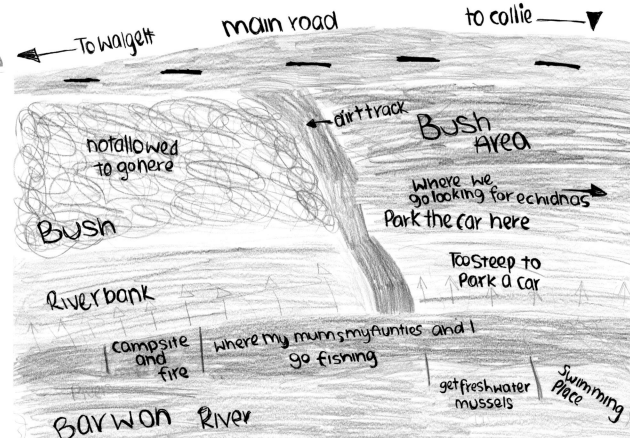

We make a fire, then dig a hole next to it, and we use the coals from the fire and put some in the hole, and we wrap the porkeypine in foil or something, and then we put it in the hole, and put more coals around it and on top, and then we put a log of fire over the top of the porkeypine. It'd take a couple of hours to cook – it depends how big it is, and how fatty.

Sometimes, too, we make damper. And when my nan was alive and we went fishing with her, she used to make us Johnny cakes over the fire. We don't really do that any more 'cause Mum can't really make Johnny cakes as well as Nan used to, so we just make damper.

There's logs along the river, and sometimes, if we're not going fishing, we go swimming there as well. Normally when we go fishing *and* swimming, me and my older cousins, we have to take the little ones down to this place on the river where there's like a slope, so you can easily go down to get into the river. It's really shallow there and the little kids can play there and us older kids can look after them and make sure they don't go too far out. And we make sure when we come back from swimming that they don't go near where the adults are fishing. Mum always tells me I have to be careful when I am watching the little kids.

Cubbies and toys

Most kids love to make cubbies, but in Aboriginal culture the play camp was a traditional part of every home. Whenever families stopped and set up camp, there was always a special area where kids built their own small windbreaks or shelters. This was close enough for parents to hear if there was trouble or danger, but far enough away for kids to be able to have some privacy.

In the play camps, boys and girls acted out events and even ceremonies that they observed in the grown-ups' camp. This was a way of learning about the roles that they would have when they grew up. They also ate snacks that they themselves provided: berries and yams, fruit and chewing gum, and even lizards or birds that they barbecued over their own fires.

Because Aboriginal families stayed at the same waterholes and meeting areas over many generations, children had a sense of long tradition about their play camps, which were built in the same place year after year, decade after decade, century after century.

In the play camps, children had all sorts of toys and playthings which they made for themselves out of the rich resources that the bush provided.

Lengths of vine were twisted together to make skipping ropes. String, made from hair or fur, was used for spinning toys or for games of 'cat's cradle'. Spinning tops were made from seeds and gourds, from beeswax and from clay. Balls were made out of paperbark and feathers, animal skins, dried grass and palm fronds. Pebbles and seeds and bones were used for games similar to marbles and jacks.

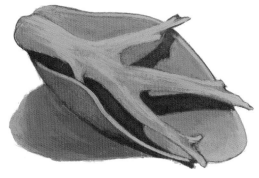

Little girls loved to play with dolls. They made 'babies' out of forked sticks and carried them about in toy coolamons. Bigger branches were turned into toddler-dolls, which were big enough to sit on hips or shoulders. These 'children' naturally always had the right skin names.

In the play camps, very young children cooked up snacks on their own little fires. Wik-Mungkan children on western Cape York (Queensland), 1933.

When large groups of people met up with each other for ceremonial occasions, kids swapped games, or passed on the latest craze in toys. When the families moved on to other campsites, the playthings went back into the bush. There would be plenty of new ones at the next home.

After Europeans came, Aboriginal kids quickly included new materials into their toys and new ideas into their games. Girls started to make dolly-dollies out of bottles, and boys began to make toy guns and horses out of anything and everything that was available.

These days, Aboriginal kids have toys bought in shops. However, they continue to use their imaginations and ingenuity to create their own playthings. And cubbies are still as popular as ever.

Tommy Kngwarraye Thompson is a Kaytetye Elder. He lives in a community called Artarre, in Central Australia. As he sits outside and tells his story into a tape recorder, he is watching children who are playing in their own campsite or 'cubbyhouse'. He describes how 'The Dreamtime lays out the "rules" for the way boys and girls play'.

Children have played in cubbyhouses since the Dreamtime. This is how we played when we were little kids and how the first Kaytetye children used to play. We all used to gather together – my big sisters, my brothers and my younger siblings. When I was a kid we stayed in the cubbies with the bigger kids looking after us.

In the same way that children from the Dreamtime played, these kids play today...

In the hot part of the day, after playing outside or at the creek, they go back and sit in their cubbyhouses – their pretend humpies, bough shelters and windbreaks – that they build close to the main camp.

[At their cubbyhouses] they have little fires too. They light small clumps of grass and pass the fire along to other cubbyhouses. They stay warm all through the winter. All through winter and summer they stay in their cubbyhouses. They play in their cubbyhouses for a while and then they go and swim in the creek. The next morning they go straight to their cubbyhouses, then swim, and go back to the cubbyhouses again.

Tamara, Amelia and Deborah all come from Walgett, in north-west New South Wales. They talk about the area at the back of Namoi Village, where they all have family. In the bush, there are cubbies as well as lots of dirt-bike tracks. Tamara's map shows some of the good places to play.

When we were a bit younger we used to go out there to the bush, and make cubbyhouses out of sticks and stuff, between the trees. There'd be boys as well as girls, all our cousins, and we made heaps of cubbies. We made a tree house too. We took the bonnet of a car up into the tree to make the wall of the tree house, and we took planks of wood up for the floor. And we took a little barbecue thing up there – we made a fire and we cooked eggs and sausages and stuff, up in the tree house.

There's bike tracks all through the bush too, and motor-bike jumps. Us girls ride bikes, as well as the boys – we've got our own bikes.

And after it rains, Walgett kids put on old clothes and go and have mud fights out there. And we make a big mud slide down the bank, into the river. So we can slide down, and then jump in and wash all the mud off.

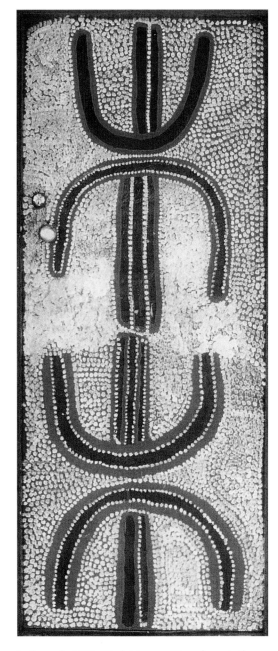

In the early 1980s Warlpiri men at Yuendumu in the Northern Territory painted thirty doors at the community school, to pass on the wisdom of Law-stories to children. This door, painted by Larry Jungarrayi Spencer, depicts a story about two uninitiated boys playing with toy spears and targets on the open plain near Kirrirdi waterhole.

Don Ross grew up in the 1920s with the other Kaytetye boys on Neutral Junction Station near Barrow Creek (Northern Territory). These kids could turn an old matchbox into a dice. Although they had never been to school, they could add numbers at lightning speed.

We used to play this racecourse game, with sticks and matchboxes, too. We'd make a round mark in the dirt, for a racecourse, sometimes a big one, if there was a mob of us. We used sticks for horses, and we marked off the track in sections. Anyhow, you'd spin the box, and if it came down straight, that was a six, and on the side a little bit, that was a three, and if it came down flat on the match side, that was one. You'd count the numbers, what came up on your box, to make your horse go round the track. We used to name the horses by the ones we used to ride.

Wik-Mungkan children in western Cape York use cuttlefish to make a miniature campsite, 1935.

Lena Crabbe grew up in the 1920s in the south-west of Western Australia. Her mother was very ill from tuberculosis, so Lena had to spend most of her time looking after her six younger brothers and sisters.

When I did have time to play I liked to make bush toys, especially little bush dolls. We'd get the nuts off the trees, give them smaller gumnuts for boobs, stick a bit of wool on their head for hair, and wrap little rags around them for a dress. We had a lot of fun with them. The boys would make matchbox trolleys, like carts, and pull them around and sometimes we'd put our little dolls in their carts and have a game that way.

Alice Bilari Smith describes the games she played when she was growing up in the Pilbara (Western Australia) during the 1930s.

We just wander round and play most of the time, all the young girls. We used to be nine girls: Hilda, Leary, Dulcie, Trixie, Mabel, me, Amy, Joyce and Dora Gilba, all of us together going round like that.

...We only played with sticks and rocks – that's all we used to play with. We might make a yard with all the rocks, and make a little bit of island or something. That's all we used to do... We used to get a stick... then put a bridle on the head part with some sort of string, then run around with that, chasing one another. We ride that one, and we used to gallop – but by running, not the stick!

We used to play fighting, too. We used to get little waddies. All the girls would fight with the waddy, and all the boys with a spear – blunt one, you know, not a sharp spear. Sometimes they used to spear us! We used to guard it with the waddy! We used to play that one, but they used to blunt that thing first, then it was all right.

Right: A boy at Borroloola (Northern Territory) concentrates hard as as he makes himself a toy, 1992. While a single tin can is often attached to a wire handle to make a toy called a 'tracker', a 'truck', a 'roller' or a 'motor-car', two or more cans can be joined to make a road train.

Above right: Three boys at Momega Outstation, Maningrida (Northern Territory), show off their home-made motor-cars, 1980.

When Ian Abdulla was growing up along the River Murray in the 1950s, his family would sometimes make an inexpensive meal by boiling up a sheep's head, bought from the slaughter yards. With a bit of imagination, the bone could be recycled.

When all the meat was eaten off the head... us boys would play cowboys and Indians with the jawbone of the sheep's head, which was a cheap way of getting a toy gun. We would break limbs from the trees to use as horses because the leaves would make a lot of dust, just like teams of horses coming towards each other.

Kain comes from Macksville on the north coast of New South Wales. Currently in Year 11 at a Sydney boarding school, Kain describes himself as 'a techie'.

I do a lot of stuff with computers, when I get a chance. I built my own computer, which normally would've cost about $2000 but if you build it yourself it reduces the price down to about $800. The joy you get from that is that you've actually made something yourself and you know how it works, and if something goes wrong, you can find out how to fix it.

Back home, I help a lot of family and friends with their computers. I really like figuring out a problem, struggling with it and overcoming it.

Playing sport

In traditional society, the country itself was a vast adventure playground, used for all sorts of games. Trees were for climbing, hills were for rolling down, and the bush provided cover for hide-and-seek. In open areas, games similar to blind-man's buff and statues were played, and of course tag and chasings were always very popular.

As well as these informal games that kids loved, there were also various organised games. These were regarded as important ways for young people to develop the reflexes and physical fitness that were needed for hunting. In some team games, there were up to fifty a side, and adults sometimes played alongside children. Competition was fierce, but there weren't any prizes. Sport, like ceremony, was a way for the community to come together.

One very popular game, known by many different names across the continent, was so similar to Australian Rules football that some historians believe AFL is derived from this Indigenous game. Another ball game, similar to hockey, was played on the islands of the Torres Strait as well as on the mainland. The sticks were made from young saplings which had a hooked root.

When Europeans brought new games to the continent, Indigenous people took them over. On the missions and reserves, sporting contests provided a way for people to get together. And in many Aboriginal communities today, the football season is the time when families travel and meet up, as they once used to do for ceremony.

Walmajarri man Peter Skipper grew up during the 1930s. He describes playing a traditional game in which a ball, called a *turlurlu*, was bowled by one team, and members of the opposing team used their fighting sticks like cricket bats, to hit it away.

This story is about a game we called *turlurlu*, which we used to play in the Great Sandy Desert where we lived. It was a popular game, rather like a game white people play when they throw or knock a ball around in a playing field. We used to throw this thing we called a *turlurlu* on the open flat. Men and boys used to play that game, it was a big thing. Girls and women didn't play it, only men did. The older men used that game for teaching the young men and boys to throw accurately. We played it again and again as a form of training in the desert. This is how we lived; this is how we were taught. It wasn't just a game, it was an important way of learning.

Kaytetye Elder Tommy Kngwarraye Thompson describes a traditional game called *peltye*, which was similar to football.

People have played *peltye* since the Dreamtime. In the Dreamtime that's how people amused themselves when they were full after having a good feed of meat or *ahakeye* (bush plums) or maybe sugarbag or perhaps yams, or splitjack fruit.

They stayed at the camp then and played *peltye* just for fun. They threw the hair-string ball amongst themselves as a way of having fun. That's what they did. It was the game played by our ancestors.

Matt and Andrew are cousins who have grown up in Sydney's inner south-west.

On Friday nights we always have games of touch football. It's just however many turn up – boys aged from twelve or thirteen up to eighteen or nineteen. To set up the teams, we just mix it up. Sometimes dads come along and get involved, and we have a mixed side. Or they might organise it. It just always happens on Friday nights at Redfern Oval. There's no ref or umpire or anything – we just call it both ways. It's probably more competitive than actual team games, 'cause we're all close. We've all been around each other since we were little kids. We've got a good bond with each other, and most of us are related.

Playing football at a Town in the River Land and the colour of each team were Renmarck blue and white and Gerard Mission in the sixty's were purple and white.

Artist Ian Abdulla played Australian Rules football as a teenager in the 1960s, when he was growing up in the Murray River area. His team, from Gerard Mission, was all Aboriginal.

In the note at the top of the painting, Ian explains that his team colours were purple and white. At this particular match, the opposition team from the town of Renmark were blue and white.

Margaret Tucker describes various games played at Cummeragunja Mission in the early years of the twentieth century. She begins with an account of the young people playing hockey (with home-made sticks) against the missionaries.

When the game became faster, we yelled orders, weaving in and out of each other's way, hitting the ball up to the goal. The excitement was too much. We would forget the missionaries, and a few swear words would come out in the heat of the moment. Everyone would gasp at the culprit, then look at the missionaries. We knew our game of hockey was over for the day... When the sticks and balls were collected by the missionaries, we would play rounders and cricket and even football with rag balls sewn together by an older sister or parent...

Everyone was allowed to play rounders and our parents would join in too. They would bat and a young one would do the running for them...

Football was hilarious. There were not enough boys so girls made up the number. A grown-up would umpire the match, usually one of our wags, who would give the girls free kicks and favours. Halfway through the match the opposition would give chase to the waggish umpire and give him a rough time. It would all end in good humour, from what I can remember.

By the 1930s, when Isabel Flick was growing up on the reserve at Collarenebri, English games such as rounders were popular. In this account Isabel shows how the Elders would use one of the new games as a way to hold all the groups of the community together.

And then there was Kenny Mundy and Granny Fanny, they used to get out there on Sundays, every Sunday, and they'd have a game of rounders going... One week it'd be the kids playing the grown-ups, then it might be married versus singles, and the next week it'd be the boys playing the girls, little girls right up to the oldest – and the oldest person had to bat, always had to bat, and they had to bat first. And we played rounders for hours, you know.

Above: Tiwi children waiting for a game, Bathurst Island (Northern Territory), 1988.

Top right: Hip hop style is melded into the traditional Indigenous sporting culture.

Below: In this photograph taken at a Vibe festival, three games of 3on3 basketball are happening on one court.

The issue of racism in sport gets into the news all too often. While this happens at the professional level, racist behaviour also occurs in amateur and even junior sport.

In June 2010, Aboriginal footballer Timana Tahu left the State of Origin team after the white coach made racist comments about an Aboriginal player from the opposing team. Seventeen-year-old Tjimarri Sanderson-Milera from South Australia wrote a letter to the *Koori Mail*, relating this incident to the racism he himself had experienced as a young athlete.

As a young Aboriginal sports player I have experienced racism. When I first joined a club about six years ago with my two cousins, we were sitting down watching because we were too shy to participate at first.

A parent member called the police complaining that we were 'hanging around the club probably looking to go through people's bags'. Seeing Aboriginal kids at the club, her first assumption was that we were there to steal, and that we were not members of the club and were not there for genuine reasons.

Having experiences like this, it feels good to see a sportsperson who is at a high level making a stand for his culture and being proud of who he is.

Timana Tahu said, 'I believe I am a role model for children and I did this to show my kids that this type of behaviour is wrong.' By doing this for his own kids he also represents all young Aboriginal people.

Vibe 3on3® is a travelling basketball and hip hop festival that was first held in the Western Australian community of Broome in 1999 and has now been held in regional centres across the continent on over a hundred occasions.

Mayrah Sonter, who produces Vibe 3on3® for Vibe Australia, talks about how young people are drawn to the festival.

We always say there's one rule at the Vibe 3on3 – and that is that you have to have fun!

The game of 3on3 basketball originated in the hip hop style of street ball in the States. Kids in remote Indigenous communities are very much in tune with the latest hip hop fashions, songs and dance crazes, and so it really appeals to them.

We do ten festivals a year in different communities. People log on to our website and ask us, if they want us to come and put on a free day for the kids, and the local community help us to organise it from the ground – they have the local knowledge.

In addition to the basketball there are art lessons and lessons in hip hop dancing and breakdancing, and the local Aboriginal Medical Service always has a stall.

Sometimes we'll bring along rappers and they'll rap with the kids, and we take a DJ with us, who plays music through the whole event, and health messages are also played over the sound system.

We're there to encourage the kids to have a healthy lifestyle and say NO to drugs and all that sort of thing, but we're also there to break down the shame-factor that a lot of kids in Indigenous communities have, and we do that by role-modelling. We take away a fully Indigenous staff of about twelve people, and we encourage the kids and show them how it's done. And the older kids in turn really encourage the younger kids. I think that's something inherent in Indigenous communities – the extended kinship of family that means big kids help younger kids.

Throwing and passing a ball has always been a skill that most Indigenous kids have, and the beauty of the Vibe 3on3 is that everyone can get in and give it a go. The kids run their own games – we don't put people on the court with them and ref them. They learn how to interact well with each other and not get into fights, and it always just runs smoothly.

Playing in the water

Whether their traditional homeland was on the coast or inland, Aboriginal kids always loved to play in water. Even in dry country, there was usually a waterhole where kids could paddle or swim. Sometimes a big puddle was good enough!

Children who lived near rivers or the sea learned to swim almost as soon as they learned to walk. There were competitions to see who could swim fastest, who could dive best, and who could stay under water the longest. All of these games were a way to practise skills needed for getting bush tucker – whether mussels or waterlily, crayfish or file snakes or ducks.

Toy boats were also very popular, and in some places children had their own miniature canoes or rafts. Chucking mud balls and making mud slides was another way to have fun.

As always in traditional life, freedom was linked to knowledge and responsibility. Grown-ups or big kids kept an eye on youngsters, until they knew how to be safe in the water. Stories of scary river monsters such as the bunyip were used to warn kids away from deep holes and strong currents – and from sacred places.

When Aboriginal people started living on missions and reserves, there was usually no water supply provided. In these circumstances, playing in a nearby creek or river was a way to have fun and keep clean at the same time. However, children were taught never to play near the water that was used for drinking.

In some country towns, such as Moree in northern New South Wales, the local authorities did not let Aboriginal kids swim with the white kids in the municipal swimming pool. In 1965 a group of university students, led by Arrernte man Charles Perkins, travelled to Moree, where they led a protest to win the right for everyone to swim in the baths.

Rita Huggins describes how, even at the mission at Cherbourg (Queensland) in the 1930s, the kids would still have fun in the water.

After school we would wander off to the local swimming place known as the Bogey Hole at Barambah Creek. In summer this place would attract the kids in droves, seeking out the cool water. Most of us would strip off and dive straight in. The boys preferred to climb out on the thick limbs of the tree and show off their different styles of diving. They all made sure that the girls they liked would be watching. Sometimes we would drift down on logs, splashing, singing and skylarking away. The younger children often came with us and it was our duty to look after them. We might only have been ten years old but we were guardians to a bunch of babies. We would make sure that they had as much fun as we did... The older children would take them home, whether or not they were their brothers and sisters. It was always like that when I was growing up. We had such a deep sense of loving for each other.

Left: At Iapidi Iapin waterhole (near Ramingining, Northern Territory), boys take turns to bomb down into the water.

For kids like Sandy Atkinson, who grew up on Cummeragunja Mission in the 1930s, swimming the wide and dangerous Murray River was an unofficial initiation rite.

Living on the banks of the Murray River we could go and spend lots and lots of time in the summertime swimming, and everyone would become great swimmers. One of the initiation parts of kids' [lives] would be your first swim across the Murray. And I can remember there was a great snag – a tree that fell down, and it almost went to the middle of the river... So you'd cheat, in a way, and get out to the very edge of that tree. And then you'd swim, and you wouldn't have a great length to swim across. But once you swam the Murray, then you felt you was in the big league.

June Barker explains how kids learned to keep safe, as well as to swim.

Right down along the Barwon–Darling River, there was always a *mirrioola* or *mirrigunnah* in the waterholes. In the Murray River, a bunyip or the little *bekka* people were waiting. All these mythical beings prevented children from coming to some harm or straying too far away. This was Aboriginal way of warning their children of danger. It prevented children from getting drowned in the waterholes or lost in the bush.

This famous photograph of Aboriginal activist Charles Perkins with children in the swimming pool at Moree was first published in the national newspaper, the *Australian*, in 1965.

By highlighting racial segregation, it drew public attention to the discrimination that Aboriginal people suffered in the areas of education, housing, health and employment.

Betty Lockyer was born on the Beagle Bay Mission (Western Australia) in 1942. When she was five her family moved south to Broome, to live with relatives. Their home was in the part of town known as Chinatown.

Down the marsh where we lived with Uncle Jacob and Aunty Kudjie, there were four houses built on stilts. They were built on stilts because the high tides would flood the marsh basin, which in turn would overflow into the streets, shops and houses. Some houses would have sea water coming up through the floorboards and doors...

During the day when it was big tide, we'd dive from the windows and steps straight into the swirling waters, having the time of our lives, yelling and screaming, ducking and diving, holding our breath and swimming underwater. We'd also fish from the windows, catching whiting and small bream. Other people would try catching fish with their nets. On weekends we'd beg our mums and dads to let us go fishing down at the big jetty. Big Jetty (at Town Beach) was taboo for us. Our parents had to take us themselves or with trusted people. Never were we allowed to go there by ourselves...

Streeter Jetty was the small jetty which the luggers used for refuelling, picking up stores and equipment, and when the crew got off for a spell from the sea.

We loved swimming down there. Most of the Chinatown kids swam, fished or just plain played there. Even when the tide went out we'd play on the beach or in the mangroves, looking for *bugulbugul* or mud skippies, sea snakes and cockles. We didn't play in the mangroves when it got dark for fear of the *goonboons* – scary hairy creatures who loved to eat kids. They were ugly and short. We never heard of big tall *goonboons*.

Most of us kids were fortunate to live in Chinatown.

These kids from the desert are having fun in the salt water during a holiday at Tathra on the New South Wales south coast, 2004.

In the 1980s Irene Jimmy described a special way of having fun on the Victoria River at Kalkaringi (Northern Territory).

One of our favourite things to do in the river is to build a slippery slide. You need a lot of kids to make the slide big enough. Usually we choose a steep bank that leads into the river... We wet the dry clay along the water's edge and rub it with our hands until it is smooth and slippery. Then we take off most of our clothes and rub ourselves with mud from the river. It feels great to have wet, slippery mud from the river all over your body on a hot day. Once the slide is ready – really smooth and slippery – and our bodies are all wet and slippery, we take it in turns to run very fast towards the slide and then slip along it. Sometimes we stay on our feet but usually we slide along on our backs. It is fun, especially when a few kids are sliding at once and we get all tangled up.

We play lots of games in the water, too. When our uncles or older cousins come to the river with us we play somersaulting games. We stand in their cupped hands and they fling us straight up in the air. I can do one and a half somersaults before I hit the water.

Kim Holten grew up in the Sydney suburb of La Perouse in the 1960s. Her story is about diving for money, but the skills that she learned from her older cousins were the same skills that these kids' ancestors would have used in order to dive for crayfish or abalone. And while the 'catch' was converted into shop food, it was shared traditional way.

Growing up at La Perouse, there would be *all* of us – steps and stairs – and the bigger ones would always look after the smaller ones, and it didn't matter if we were blood-related or not, we were all cousins.

We'd go off down to the beach and dive off the wharf for pennies, shillings, sixpences and threepences – stick 'em in our gobs. And without the big kids showing me where to put the money, I wouldn't have been able to do that. And I wouldn't have been able to dive as well as I do today, without them showing me how to hold my breath and kick my legs.

See, loads of American tourists used to come down to Lapa because old Joe Timbery used to throw the boomerang up the top of the tram loop, and then a bit further down the road there was Johnny Cann's snake show. And when these tourists used to come round the bottom of the loop, they'd see all us kids swimming off the wharf, and we'd sing out 'Chuck us a deener!' Or we might ask for a shilling or even two bob.

So they would throw the coins into the water – it was mainly threepences or sometimes only pennies, but at least you couldn't choke on a penny! – and kids would dive off the wharf, or we'd already be in the water, looking up. And wherever the money went, there'd be all these bottoms, and legs kicking.

So you'd go down – the water was quite clear there, around the wharf – and you'd pick the coin up and then you'd come back up and wave it at the tourist, and they'd clap, and then you'd put the coin in your cheek so you wouldn't lose it – 'cause you had nowhere else to put it! – and you'd wait for the next one.

And then at the end of the day, as the sun was setting over Botany Bay, we'd pool all the money and we'd go to the Paragon and get a big bag of chips and a big bottle of lemonade, a loaf of *un*-cut bread, and we'd rip the top off the loaf, take the guts out – the soft part – and share that, and then we'd stuff the loaf with the chips, and pass it round with the cousins and the sisters and the brothers that were there. Pass it round, pass it round.

Learning through song and ceremony

Most Australians are used to seeing Aboriginal dancers at cultural events, whether in real life or on television.

While Aboriginal people are proud to showcase their culture, their dances aren't just about entertainment. Traditionally, music and dance were used to tell sacred stories in religious ceremony. The words of the songs and the movements of the dancers brought the Law-stories to life.

In the rituals of many religions, there are different roles for women and for men. Similarly, in traditional Aboriginal society there was separate Women's Business and Men's Business, and children were not allowed to attend certain ceremonies.

However, there were also regular occasions on which the whole community gathered. When there was an abundance of seasonal food in a particular place, families would travel vast distances and come together for celebrations that would go on for days or even weeks.

As children sat listening to the songs and watching the dances unfold, it was like seeing a docu-drama of their own history. The words seeped into their memories, helping them to know the Law.

Just as kids play-acted the roles of hunter or mother, they also copied the adults' ceremonies. In this way, dance steps and songs were passed on, generation after generation.

Children also liked to make their own instruments. A gum leaf was blown to make a tune, or a hollow reed was used as a whistle. Big seed pods were shaken like maraccas, and sticks were used to make a clapping sound.

These days, many young Aboriginals and Torres Strait Islanders are proudly keeping up their ceremonial traditions in dance. Even if the dance-form is contemporary, the spiritual sense remains strong. The dancers re-enact traditional practices, and re-interpret ancient stories.

From remote communities to the city, young Indigenous people are also writing and playing music. Electric guitars have taken over from gum leaves, and the music might be in the style of rock and roll, country and western or hip hop, but the words of the songs reflect Indigenous life. Young musicians find their role-models in the Aboriginal community.

Warlpiri man Darby Jampijinpa Ross describes ceremony as a way of learning.

The older people would teach Dreamings and ceremonies to the young men. They would paint them with ochre and feathers. They would say, 'We're going to teach you young fellas so you can look after your country.'

Against a backdrop of skyscrapers, dancers perform at Woggan-magule in Sydney's Botanic Gardens on Survival Day (26 January) 2009. They carry on the tradition of the ceremonies that were conducted by many generations of Aboriginal people in the place that would become the site for Australia's first city.

The group in the photo below is led by Dharpaloco, whose story appears at right. Her sister Gapala says of the dancing: 'It feels like it's meant to be in that garden.'

Gapala and Dharpaloco have family in Yirrkala (Northern Territory) and in Sydney, where they live. They are members of the contemporary Indigenous dance group Jannawi, which their mother runs.

We do contemporary Indigenous dancing. It's really fun. In the dance group, there's another girl from our school, and a few kids from La Perouse and other places in Sydney. There are boys as well as girls in the group, but we only dance with other girls. The boys do their own stuff, like kangaroo dance, and they sing songs and play the didg.

The way we dance, we have to have a meaning to it. When we are learning a new dance we sit around for a bit and our mother tells us what the story is about, and what we have to do, to dance it out. If we have an idea of our own, we show everybody. Our mum makes the costumes.

We have two main dances that we do. We have a leaf dance, which is like cleansing the earth where we dance – to get all the bad spirits away – and we have the waratah dance. It tells the story of the white waratah, and how it became red.

We do the cleansing because it sort of protects our spirit, and we wear white ochre, which also protects our spirit when we dance.

Arrernte Elder Wenten Rubuntja remembers many *altharte* ceremonies held in and around Alice Springs when he was growing up.

Us kids would watch the men and women dancing...The *altharte* was the really olden time ceremony...

They danced the *altharte* for the *ayeparenye* (caterpillar)... That *altharte* ceremony belonged to Alice Springs people... The men and women danced at the *altharte*, gathering together for the *Tywerrenge* (sacred objects, Law)... All the others from other places gathered round and watched the women and men dancing. It was really good. The women danced, and all the men would sing. And the boss man would sing the *Tywerrenge*. It was like that. Really good. We saw it as kids. The men used to dance and the little boys danced too – not the little girls – they used to dance ... with the old women. When we were small ones we used to dance. The little boys danced – and when the little girls danced they really used to go for it. Everybody used to come in from all over the place. Different languages – Alyawarr, Kaytetye, Arrernte, Luritja, Pitjantjatjara, Warlpiri, Ngaliya and all. They used to talk Arrernte to each other as well and find husbands and wives from different groups. They'd meet each other during the *altharte* ceremony time.

A young dancer from Mer (Murray Island) in the Torres Strait performs a traditional dance at the Native Title Conference in Melbourne, 2009. Mer is the homeland of Eddie Mabo, the visionary Land Rights leader who died in 1992 shortly before the High Court victory that bears his name.

The Torres Strait flag features a feathered headdress like the one this boy is wearing.

In the islands of the Torres Strait, the tradition of dance actions and dance songs is passed down from men to boys and from women to girls. Because the culture is so strong, new elements can be woven into the stories. After the arrival of Christian missionaries on 1 July 1871, people began to compose language-hymns as well as the dance songs which pass on important information about the sea and the sky and the environment.

Dancer and singer David Ned David, from Yam Island, talks about how he learned this tradition, and what it means.

Doing a dance – it's the main thing of the community. Like we sort of *grow* in it... It's been passed on from our dead ancestors down to us.

Our uncles make us stand on the side when they dance, and we dance with them, and they tell us how to go, how the action go. And when you go dancing, you dance properly – because dancing, we don't take it like a joke up in the island. It is a serious thing that is passed on... Like the dancing was the first priority.

I'll give an example. My uncle Maigun, he was dancing – and when I was a small boy in the primary school, I want to be like him. So to be like him, I've got to dance like him, and I try to be like him, and to dance like him, so that perhaps he see me and say, 'Hey, this boy can dance!'

And Uncle Maigun, I follow him because he was my role-model.

In a similar way, David Ned David picked up the songs. The term 'language' here refers to Kala Lagaw Ya, the traditional Torres Strait language of the central islands.

In my generation we didn't have anything like a TV to entertain us, so we'd just sit down with our parents and hear them as they sing a song... and we learned to sing with them, and we do that every night after dinner, we sit down and we sing the language-hymns, or even a dancing song. Sing with them – yeah!

And before Christmas or Easter or the 1st of July, there was always a gathering to learn our language-hymns....

When you sing a language-hymn or you sing a language-dance, it also tells a story about your community, and it also tells a story about your identity.

Roy Kebisu, who is also from Yam Island, learned to make the elaborate 'playthings' which Torres Strait dancers use for their music and performance.

I know how to make the playthings for the island dance. I was taught by my father and my uncle how to do them.

The playthings that we use today, they go way back – back to my grandfather's day, I suppose. The same playthings that we have today, they danced the same playthings back then.

Felicia and Selina are cousins who live in Broken Hill. They are members of the Spirit Catchers dance group, which is run by the community organisation Thankakali. Selina's brother Kym has the role of Creator in the Creation dance.

In the afternoons and on weekends we go to Thankakali. You can do stuff there like painting, sport, hygiene, and there's dancing too, so that kids get involved with their culture. We mainly do traditional dance but if we want to relax we do a bit of modern as well. One of our older cousins plays the didgeridoo, and he and Kym teach us some of the dances.

Our first dance is the Creation. At the start we are the rocks. We all sit quiet, and then as Kym calls out the names of the animals – like emu, goanna, kangaroo, brolga – we change into them. We try to think like the animals, to *be* the animals.

After that, *we* go up the back and the boys do their kangaroo dance, where they go out hunting for kangaroo. Then us girls do the berry dance – picking the berries. After that, there's the feasting.

It's very educational, really good to do. It gives us a good picture of how the stories were told in the olden days. And when we do it, we're keeping up the traditions. Our families are really proud, because we're keeping up the traditions of our ancestors.

In Arnhem Land, the tradition of ceremony continues strongly today, with events such as the annual Garma Festival. George Milpurrurru, from Arnhem Land, explains the connection between ceremony and Law.

Through ceremony we pass on our Law, we sing and dance the stories of our ancestors, our totemic heroes, so this knowledge will last forever. Some ceremonies are secret-sacred for initiated men only, last for months. Other ceremonies with women and young people too, public *bunggal* [ceremony]. All the time we taking ceremony, this way, that way, teaching the young people all the time, teaching them Yolngu Law, about our culture through ceremony business.

Taipan Elder Dr Tommy George was taught song and ceremony by his grandfather. Tommy – who lives near the town of Laura in Queensland – explains how traditional ceremony has been adapted to fit new circumstances.

As life goes on and changes, our dances change along with it... We started the Laura Dance Festival to show the world our culture. People come from all over the country to dance here. This used to happen in the olden days too. Aboriginal people come together from different Aboriginal country to dance.

This bark painting, 'Wubarr Ceremony', was painted in 1989 by Arnhem Land artist Thompson Yulidjirri. As well as the dancers it shows singers (at top) and musicians with clap sticks and didgeridoo.

Learning through stories and pictures

Just as Muslims have the Koran and Christians have the Bible, Aboriginal people have their sacred stories which they have been telling for thousands of years.

In English, these stories are often called Dreaming stories, but they are not bedtime tales to send little children to sleep. In Aboriginal culture, these stories are the Law. They tell how the country was created and how the animals and people came into being. Most importantly, they set out the rules showing people how to behave towards each other and the land. Sometimes these stories have sad or frightening endings, because they show what happens when people break the Law.

Although children were traditionally brought up on these Law-stories, they were only told the outside layers. As they grew older, they learned more of the inside story.

Many of the stories told to children explain the responsibility of adults to care for children, and the duty of young people to respect their Elders. Other stories stress the importance of sharing and conservation.

As well as the sacred Law-stories, there were also some less serious tales, which children told to each other in the play camps, for generation after generation.

Stories were not told in words alone. For traditional Aboriginal people, the whole country was a multi-media artwork. The Creation and the Law were seen as being depicted in the mountains and hills, rivers and lakes. The shapes of these natural features commemorated the deeds of the ancestral heroes. As children journeyed with their families, the stories seemed to come to life around them. Today, some Elders continue to point out the footprints of the great Creator Spirit or of the animal-totem ancestors imprinted into rock.

In different ways across the continent, generations of people enhanced this natural art. In some areas, rock platforms were carved with huge figures. In other regions, caves were covered with paintings which were regularly repainted over thousands of years.

Other art was short-term. When people gathered for ceremony, the 'stage' of the dancing-ground would be decorated to enhance the drama that was to be enacted. Earth was sculpted into mounds, and coloured stones made a mosaic ground-map. Symbols painted onto the bodies of the dancers enhanced the ritual performance.

These days, Indigenous people continue to use many different mediums for their story-telling. Oral history, fiction, drama, paint, pottery, photography, film, and picture books: the thing that makes art 'Aboriginal' is not the medium but the maker.

In remote communities, children often start to learn their Law by watching and listening as family members bring stories to life on canvas. At the same time, kids learn the business of art-making – little by little.

For Indigenous children growing up in cities and towns, art is often a way to connect with the spirit of their culture.

Most importantly, stories are still told and children still love to listen to them. Tradition is passed down, as family history is woven with tales that go back deep into the memory of the land.

Uluru is a UNESCO World Heritage Site, important to people across the world. Yet for the people of the Western Desert, A̲nangu, it has a sacred meaning. This photograph shows one of the traditional owners of Uluru passing on knowledge to the younger generation. In a statement on the Department of Environment website for Uluru, the traditional owners explain:

'The world was once a featureless place. None of the places we know existed until Creator Beings, in the forms of people, plants and animals, travelled widely across the land. Then, in a process of creation and destruction, they formed the landscape as we know it today.'

When Yami Lester was growing up in his traditional Yankunytjatjara land during the 1940s, his mother and stepfather 'talked about the country', and how it came into being.

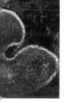

That's how they'd tell the story: they'd tell you it's real, they believed it... And I believed what they said. You couldn't doubt, it was just something real. The country wasn't just hills or creeks or trees. And it didn't feel like it was fairy tales they told me. It was real, our *kuuti*, the force that gives us life. Somebody created it, and whoever created it did it for us, so we could live and hunt and have a good time.

Paddy Japaljarri Stewart is a Warlpiri man who grew up in the Central Desert during the 1920s and 1930s. He uses the word '*Jukurrpa*' to express the idea of Law that non-Indigenous people often call 'the Dreaming'. Paddy begins by saying that this is 'the story about *Jukurrpa*' that 'they used to learn... in the old ways... from their grandparents'.

My father's grandfather taught me the first, and after a while my father taught me the same way as his father told *Jukurrpa*, and then my father is telling the same story about what his father told him, and now he's teaching me how to live on the same kind of *Jukurrpa* and follow that way what my grandfather did, and then what my father did, and then I'm going to teach my grandchildren the same way as my father taught me...

My Dreaming is the kangaroo Dreaming, the eagle Dreaming and budgerigar Dreaming, so I have three kinds of Dreamings in my *Jukurrpa* and I have to hang onto it. This is what my father taught me, and this is what I have to teach my son, and my son has to teach his sons the same way my father taught me, and that's the way it will go on from grandparents to sons, and follow that *Jukurrpa*.

No one knows when it will end.

When people were moved to missions, they still kept the stories alive. Olive Jackson decribes the storytelling at Cummeragunja.

Cummera was a place where all the Koori families were together and we kept to a lot of our old ways. The Elders would sit around the campfire at night and tell the children the old Koori stories, like the one about the hairy *bekkas*, scary little kind of people that grabbed children if they disobeyed their Elders and stayed away from the campfire at night. They'd teach us about the laws, like respecting each other and the land, and always sharing everything we had.

Matt's mother is Wiradjuri. Like Matt himself, she grew up in south-west Sydney. From her, Matt has gained a strong sense of tradition.

Mum basically taught me everything. To respect everyone, to respect the Elders, to treat everyone how you would like to be treated. She told me stories about the family – history and stuff.

When I have kids I'd get Mum to tell them stories, but I'd tell them stories as well – about my childhood, teaching them good morals, and about respecting the Elders. And I'd want them to get involved in the dancing, like I did, and community experiences. I'd want to teach them their own knowledge – like I was taught.

Aboriginal art is not done just for art's sake. Naminapu Maymaru is an artist and teacher from Yirrkala. Her father, Nänyin Maymaru, was also famous for his bark paintings. For this family, passing on the art tradition is about preserving Law, country and culture.

My father said when he became sick, 'I want all you girls... to keep on painting and to keep our culture going for the sake of me and for the sake of the country.' And that was his last word...

It's not only for me, but it's really important for us to teach our *djamarrkuli* (children) too, so that the *djama* (work) will continue passing it on, so that we don't have to lose that *rom* (law).

My clan design... can't be changed. My children will paint it the same. My father painted exactly the same design. It's not got to be changed, got to be exactly the same. We have to follow the steps. As you learn, bit by bit, you have to follow on, the rule says. As you get better, if you're really good at it, you've got all these things, designs, stored up.

Above left: The walls of this cave on the New South Wales central coast are covered with hand-stencils.

Left: Suzanne Kukika Edwards (left) and two friends at Ernabella (South Australia) in 1995 are drawing in the sand as they tell stories to each other. This is a traditional way of telling stories.

Right: Two daughters of the painter Clifford Possum Tjapaltjarri assist their father with the background for one of his canvases, Alice Springs, 1989.

Tess Napaljarri Ross is a Warlpiri Elder from Yuendumu in the Western Desert. She was part of a project at Yuendumu School in the 1980s, when traditional Law was painted onto the school doors. She describes how and why the old way was adapted to the new.

Many people told the children about the Dreamtime by drawing on the ground and on paper. They told them a long time ago in the bush by drawing on their bodies, on the ground and on the rocks. This was the way men and women used to teach the children. Now when children are at school, at a white place, [the Elders] want to pass on to them their knowledge about this place. They want them to keep and remember it. They want them to learn both ways – European and Aboriginal. They want them to see the designs, the true Dreaming, so they can follow it on the land, hills, and on the shields, boomerangs, nulla nullas, spear-throwers and on other things.

Kim Holten was raised in Sydney by her grandmother, a Dhanggati woman, who was a wonderful storyteller. A qualified teacher, Kim is now an Aboriginal Education Support Officer. Describing her grandmother as 'the great teacher' who inspired her to follow a career in education, Kim explains that the Aboriginal way of learning is to do with 'the way we communicate'.

And it's not just about the speaking but it's about the deep listening – it's being able to listen very closely to what people are saying. That was one of the invaluable lessons that my grandmother taught me, through the way she told her stories.

My aunty Boronia does it, even to this day. If she wants you to listen to her, she'll talk to you on her drawing breath in – it's like a whisper – so you have to get closer to her. And my grandmother would do that too, so it would force you to come close and lean in and listen, to really get the message – to get the meaning behind what she was saying, as that story was being built up and built up and built up and built up and built up! And then getting to the *point*, and the inflexion in the voice going down.

And the repetition of the storytelling, and the changes in the story, really make you grasp the point of sharing that knowledge and learning from what is being said.

You know, before my grandmother died, I was twenty-one, twenty-two, and I would come home from a club and I'd jump into bed with her and say, 'Come on, Ma! Tell me a story about when *you* were young.'

Yes, being able to coax those old people into telling you stories that have no relation to you in the *moment*, but they *do*, later on – those lessons, they're just *so* valuable. And that deep listening that comes through the way they tell the stories!

These days, some Aboriginal people pass on traditional stories in the form of picture books.

The photograph below, taken in Cairns in 2009, shows author-illustrator Arone Meeks at the re-launch of his award-winning picture book, *Enora and the Black Crane*, first published in 1991. Arone is holding the book as he stands next to a piece of the original artwork for the book.

At the launch party Arone said that he originally heard the story of Enora from his grandfather: 'My grandfather was a Kuku Midiji man from Laura, so it's an important story that his father told him, that was passed on to me. I did it in such a way that children could copy the illustrations very easily, and also to parallel with elements of traditional culture by using traditional colours.'

During the Land Rights struggles of the early 1970s, Bronwyn Penrith was part of a group of young urban Aboriginal people who became involved in a radical type of storytelling. Bronwyn links this to traditional methods.

The corroboree tells a story through gestures, and it signifies certain things that affect the everyday lives of the people who are watching. And I don't think it's a far step from that to telling a story with actors.

I think TV is a fantastic medium to get our messages across, but I also saw the impact that street theatre had, back in 1972, '73. I remember [the actor] Bob Maza was living in Redfern at that time, and his house became a kind of hub for all of us young ones to go to and just sit around and sing, and talk about politics. And from that came the idea of acting out some of the issues in streets and parks, when there was a demonstration on.

One performance we did was for *Four Corners*. I was dressed up as a white woman, in a gaudy dress and with white flour on my face, and I had an umbrella with words on it like 'MINING COMPANIES' and 'MULTINATIONAL INTERESTS'. Other people were demonstrating against me. And then there were the police. They were blackfellas too, but they had white masks on.

That was the only way we could get on TV at that time and get our voice heard – by getting out on the streets.

Leah Purcell is one of many Aboriginal people using a variety of new media for storytelling. Leah is well known as an actor on stage and screen, and has written books and scripts as well as her autobiographical stage-show, *Box the Pony*.

It's very empowering for us to be telling our stories through this new medium of film and television. As Aboriginal people, we know that our stories evolve, and I just hope that the wider community understands that when we speak of the Dreamtime, we're not just talking about the mythology that happened a long long time ago, but we're talking about yesterday, and today.

As well as the important stuff that must be handed on to make tradition and culture survive, there's also the fun side of who we are. And that's one of the things I try to show through my writing, through the stuff that I act, and through things like *Box the Pony*. They're all contemporary yarns, that are absolutely relevant to who we are as Indigenous people today.

In the past, a story was painted on a rock wall, and of course with time it's deteriorated due to the weather, but if we can put our stories on film, it's going to be more accessible to our young people.

Kids today are so into technology, that if they see something painted onto a rock wall, they don't find the significance to it – unless it's their name and it says they were there! So if we can make a story in a way that interests them, they feel a part of it. And they don't know it, but they're continuing on something that is ancient – and that's the passing on of our stories.

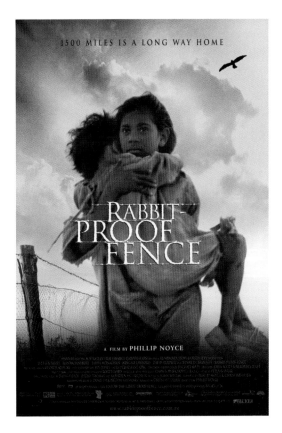

1500 MILES IS A LONG WAY HOME

RABBIT-PROOF FENCE

A FILM BY PHILLIP NOYCE

The 2002 film *Rabbit-Proof Fence*, based on the book by Doris Pilkington Garimara, told a true story about how three young Stolen Children made their escape back to their homes and families.

Born in 1990, Jaleesa Donovan has grown up in the Sydney suburb of Bankstown. On her father's side she is descended from Dhanggati and Gumbaynggirr people of the New South Wales north coast. She is currently running an oral history project with Elders who also live in the Bankstown area. Jaleesa begins by explaining why she is doing it.

Ever since I can remember I've always attended NAIDOC and other Aboriginal events, but in primary school I never really knew what 'Aboriginal' meant, because I was just who I was. I think towards the end of high school I started realising a lot of things. I didn't like history at high school, so I'd just sit there and I wouldn't really listen, but when it came to Aboriginal history, I'd actually listen.

I never really knew what the Stolen Generation was until I was learning about it in class, and I was like, 'Wow, I can't believe those things actually happened!' And there were stories coming out, like *Rabbit-Proof Fence*, about the kids being taken away. So I realised that that's why there's this *thing* between Aboriginal people and white Australia.

And I think that kind of gave me the urge to start researching and knowing about why *my* family is like it is, and what the Aboriginal history of Australia is – not just the white history. So that's what kind of brought me to this project.

Jaleesa is now funded through the Bankstown Youth Development Service to work three days a week, interviewing Elders and editing the interviews into both a DVD and a publication.

And I *love* it. To me, it isn't like a boring history thing because I actually get to speak to the Elders, and first-hand hear their experiences, whereas in history textbooks you don't get to hear the Elders' stories.

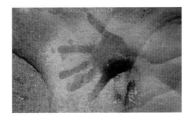

Personally, I want to share my culture, and it's hard to share your culture as a story just from one person, so it's good being able to interview all these Elders and get all these different stories to share, so people can learn – because we still have a lot of racism today. Like, Bankstown is very multicultural, but there's still that barrier coming from a few people, and I just want people to realise why Aboriginal people live the way they do, and do the things they do. I want people to learn and *understand*.

If people would understand our culture through this project, that would make me so happy – to think that I'd done something to help people understand my people and where they've come from.

For the Elders themselves, I want them to know that they are acknowledged in our community, and that their lives are very significant, and we honour them.

And for their families, I want this to be something they can keep in years to come, something they can show their kids, to say this is what they went through. So I want to be educating our people as well.

A lot of my cousins – they're very *family* orientated, and they know their culture, but I don't think they know their ancestors' culture – they just know about their culture today. But it's majorly important, I think, for people to know where they're from, who they are – and linking with other cultures as well, because we're all different, but we all have a lot in common as well. Yeah, I get really passionate about that!

Jaleesa interviewing Bankstown Elder Colin Williams, 2010.

Growing up

As children grow up, they are expected to take on greater responsibilities, until they become adults.

Traditionally, as an Aboriginal boy started to reach adolescence, his education would be taken over by his uncles. As well as learning how to hunt large animals, he would join other boys the same age for the process of initiation. The first stage of this difficult training lasted for a month or more. Boys were introduced to deeper levels of the Law, and their endurance and bravery were tested. When the initiation finished, everyone joined the celebration. Afterwards, boys left their family camp and went to live at the young men's camp.

Under traditional Law, marriages were sometimes arranged for girls when they were very young. This was to make sure that their husbands came from the right skin group, and had the wisdom and skills to be good providers. Girls stayed at their own family campsite until they were ready for marriage. As they grew older, they took a bigger role in the getting of food, and they also learned more of the secret-sacred Women's Business.

These days, young Aboriginal people wear the latest brand names and keep in touch by mobile phone or Facebook. Yet in some communities, boys still go away to 'business camp' to be initiated. Their parents are really proud when they graduate. Other boys and girls take the difficult step of leaving home and going to boarding school to complete their education.

Joining the workforce or doing a tertiary course are also rites of passage. And some young Indigenous women and men take on the responsibility of starting their own families at an early age.

Whether they live in the city or in remote communities, many young Aboriginal people play leadership roles in their schools and communities.

David Mowaljarli is from the Kimberley. He explains that the rules for inatation were made Law at the time of Creation, when the animal-ancestors were still in human form.

The flying foxes, they started the Law, and birds like the eaglehawk, bowerbird, brolga and turkey, wild ducks, all those birds, they all started the Law so we follow their tracks before they became with feathers... Then the animals, like the possums, they started the Law... those birds and animals what make the Law for initiation, we all one, and we carry on their Law, what they said when they set it up, and it is from them that we initiate one another. They were human beings first. Time came when they changed and then we carried it on and that's the Law that never will cease. It's on the Earth.

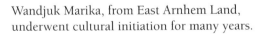

Wandjuk Marika, from East Arnhem Land, underwent cultural initiation for many years.

Then I *knew* all about life in the bush, how to behave. Do not touch anything, or muck around with anybody, or say bad words or swear… I had to learn the right behaviour and be a sensible, kind, respectable man. I study until I grew up to be a man.

Left: While the initiation process is secret, the ceremonies include celebrations by the family and community.
   In this ceremony at Nagalala, East Arnhem Land, in 1979, the four young initiates sit with mothers and aunties as well as fathers and uncles.

Jack Mirritji, from Arnhem Land, talks of the time when he became a man.

When an Aboriginal is initiated, it is like his death, and rebirth in the form of a man. The boy's spirit leaves his body and goes (symbolically) into the man...

   When I was about fourteen years old, my father's youngest brother, at that time my second father, talked with several older people to arrange my initiation... He told the older men:

   'Mirritji is old enough and it is time to teach him the way and beliefs of his father and grandfather. He must learn now about the important things of the Dreamtime so that he will start to know.'

   And the older men agreed with my father's youngest brother and they asked him what sort of *bunggal* (ceremony) he would like for my initiation. He told them he would like the *marndayala* or dog dance and he discussed that with some other people who wanted to initiate some other young men as well. Everybody agreed with the *marndayala* ceremony because in this *hunggal* all people concerned could take part in it, no matter what their Dreaming was.

Although teenage girls did not go through the kind of initiation process that young men underwent, the old women instructed them about how to behave, especially in regard to choosing a partner from the right skin group.
   Alice Bilari Smith, from the Pilbara, talks from her experience of being an adolescent in the 1940s.

They used to look after every bit of thing, the old people. No one was allowed to do the wrong thing, especially the teenagers coming up. They used to watch them properly...

   When the [girls] were about ten or eleven years old, they know about growing up. Because the old people always used to talk about things in the outside campfire – tell them how we have to do things, how you've got to go with a *nyuba* – that's a boyfriend. You find a *nyuba*, and you go with a *nyuba*, and that's your *nyuba* forever; you're going to have a family, you two fellas. And don't go with the wrong one: uncle or brother or anything like that. You're not allowed to. You've got to only go with the straight [right skin] man... Too close was no good...

   The mother was not allowed to say all those things – only the old grannies. Doesn't matter whether it's not my own grandmother, long as it's a grandmother, and they're the one who's got to tell us.

Ricky, who comes from Bowraville on the mid north coast of New South Wales, talks about why he chose to finish his schooling at a Sydney boarding school.

I'd been down to Sydney a lot with my primary school, so I wasn't too bad about coming to Sydney. But boarding school didn't sound too good.

It was my nan that talked me into it. She was saying that I should come down here because there's more resources here than the schools back home.

My nan was part of the Stolen Generation, so she *had* to go away to school. And she thought that it would be a good idea that I finish my education, but make the choice to do it, instead of getting told to do it. She just talked to me a bit about it, and she said, 'Whatever you do, it doesn't really worry me, as long as you finish school.' I said, 'All right,' and I chose to come down.

I've had two cousins come through here. One brother finished last year and I've got another brother here now, so that makes it easier. And I'm not too bad at making friends.

Jade is from the Biripi nation. He has grown up near Taree, on the north coast of New South Wales, and is in Year 10 at school. He likes swimming, fishing, playing football, and spending time with his friends and family.

Where I come from, Aboriginal culture is acted out through the things we do. Like fishing, playing sport, the way us Aboriginal people socialise with each other, the way we talk, the humour, that kind of stuff. We understand each other more, know what we're saying to each other.

I've always wanted to be a police officer, so that's what I'm going to do. I'm going to go to Charles Sturt University in Wagga Wagga, and get a policing degree. I don't know if I'd want to go and work up in Queensland, or come back home and work in my own community.

But yeah – it'd be good to show younger kids that police *are* good people. And if it was an Aboriginal person who was in trouble, they'd probably listen and understand another Aboriginal person more. Like, I'd probably be able to talk some sense into them, rather than if a white person come along and try to tell them what to do, and they might end up punching each other in the head.

I'd like to show how to try to get something in life, rather than fighting. Because that won't get you anywhere.

Above: A young father, Fred Henaway, is taking his three-year-old son to the Indigenous Football Festival at Townsville, July 2009.

For any young person, growing up means working out who you are. For Aboriginal kids raised outside their community, this is often a difficult process.

Linda Burney was born in 1957 in the New South Wales Riverland. She was brought up by her great-aunt and great-uncle, who were of Scottish ancestry. While Linda knew her mother, she knew nothing about her Wiradjuri father. In this moving account Linda describes a crucial stage in her journey of growing up.

I remember spending a lot of very deep thought around the ages of twelve or thirteen about whether I was Aboriginal or not. Inherently I think I knew, but I didn't know *for sure*, because back in those days in small country towns it was still difficult to identify as an Aboriginal person. I experienced lots of teasing about it from other children, but it was also about the additional layer of being fatherless. And I'm not quite sure what people thought was worse – being Aboriginal or being illegitimate!

It was a burden that I carried with me, but not in a way that I ever let it get me down. I think that's part of my personality, part of my resilience, and somehow or other having a confidence in myself. But you know, really – coming to terms with my Aboriginality at the age of twelve or thirteen was realising that there is only one path for me, and that is the path of truth.

Mayrah Sonter was born in 1983 and grew up in Redfern, in inner Sydney. Her educational pathway shows how a contemporary young Wiradjuri woman can keep her identity strong, while seizing new opportunities.

Although by no means have I been raised in a traditional lifestyle in the city, I still have the traditional elements of always striving to be a warrior, or to be the best I can be, while adapting to my environment.

After going to preschool at Murawina, down on the Block, I went to Redfern Primary School, where I was eventually the school captain. We had a majority of Indigenous students there during my younger years, and some of the parents were prominent people in the community. I wouldn't be able to do what I do now if I didn't have that education at Redfern first.

After that, I got a scholarship to PLC [Presbyterian Ladies College, Sydney], where I went through my secondary schooling as the only Indigenous girl at the school. I didn't have anyone else there – any role-models or mentors.

But then when I went to university, I went to an Indigenous House of Learning at the university, and I got back in touch with Indigenous students like myself. And we all found that, while you might go off to school or whatever, you do always seem to come back to community.

People often ask me which side of the fence I walk on – the black side or the white side. I can walk on both sides quite well, but the thing that always comes back to me is I always do give back to community.

© HEIDE SMITH

A Tiwi schoolgirl is learning to use ochre paint and a stick to paint her friend's face. These traditional designs, worn in ceremonies, have been passed down over many generations.

Conclusion

Warlpiri Elder Molly Nungarrayi sums up a lifetime of learning from old people who in turn learned from their ancestors.

As we listen to these stories by Aboriginal and Torres Strait Islander Elders and young people, we discover some of the things that the children of this land have been doing for generation upon generation, and which they are still doing today:

> Respecting the Elders...
> Observing the Law...
> Learning from the natural world...
> Helping each other...
> Sharing the resources...
> Giving back to community...
> Having fun together...

Words wind and weave around the land, bringing past into present, and today into the future.

As we listen to the stories that come from country and from inside the heart, we find wisdom that could help us care for each other and for the land where we all now live.

We are following the *Jukurrpa* stories from our grandmothers and grandfathers, mothers and fathers. That's why we have to look after the country. We are keeping the Law strong...

We still know everything from our grandparents... We watched them and we still remember from a long time ago. Our grandparents showed us when we were children and we understand everything now because we were well educated. From the time that we were little children we learned things, right up until we grew big and became old. It was as a child that I began to learn and carry it on.

We are still holding it, we are still looking after it. Our understanding continues forever. We keep the Law eternally.

Young Dharawal man Raymond Ingrey speaks of the importance of continuing the culture.

Living in the city, we've had to find a balance. The western lifestyle, working every day, driving cars around, going to school – that's how we live. But we've kept the importance of our cultural identity and practices.

As Aboriginal people, if we lose our culture, we lose who we are and where we come from, and that's what we, as a community, don't want to happen.

The Elders have done their job in getting us this far, and the way I see it, it's up to us young ones to continue to drive it forward and make sure that we consult with them all the time, and get it right.

We're just doing our responsibility, what we've been put here to do, and that's to continue our culture, to make it strong again. We're completing our responsibility as Aboriginal people.

Yorta Yorta Elder Lola James talks about respect.

Years ago the main thing taught to children was respect. It's an old Koori tradition – respect for your Elders, respect for each other, respect for the land. This held families and communities together...

If you want respect, you've got to give it out. We need to bring that respect back to the young ones coming up now. Respect was the thing that made Koori culture strong and fair.

Tom Calma, the former Aboriginal and Torres Strait Islander Social Justice Commissioner, gives a wonderful message.

From self-respect comes dignity and from dignity comes hope. We need that hope for our young people.

Notes on the contributors

Contributors are listed alphabetically, by first name. Those under the age of eighteen at the time of their interview are listed by first name only.

Alice Bilari Smith was born in 1928 on Rocklea Station, in the north-west of Western Australia. She was raised in the traditional way by her mother, a Banyjima woman, and her Kurrama stepfather. Despite moving to the town of Roebourne, she brought up her own children to know their language and culture.

Alice Nannup was born in 1911 in the Pilbara (Western Australia). Her mother was a Yindjibarndi woman who worked on cattle stations in her traditional country. Alice's father was the white owner of the station where Alice spent most of her childhood. She grew up speaking Kariyarra and Ngarluma as well as English.

Alice Rigney is a Narangga Kaurna woman. She grew up at the Point Pearce Mission on the Yorke Peninsula (South Australia) in the 1940s. During a long and outstanding career as an educator, she became the first Aboriginal female school principal in her state. Alice Rigney was awarded a doctorate from the University of South Australia in 1998.

Andrew has grown up in an inner suburb of Sydney and is outstanding at most sports. His father is Wiradjuri and Bundjalung, and his mother is Wiradjuri. Andrew was in Year 11 at the time of his interview for this book.

Andy Tjilari is a Pitjantjatjara man whose traditional country is near Pipalyatjara in the north-west of South Australia. In 1937, when Andy was still a child, his family moved to the newly established mission at Ernabella. Andy is a *ngankari* (traditional healer) and artist as well as being an active worker for his community.

Arone Meeks was born in 1957. A Kuku Midigi man, his country is the area around Laura in north Queenland. Arone received a traditional education from his grandfather and other Elders before going to art school. His artwork is held in major Australian and international collections.

Arthur Shadforth was born in the 1960s near Borroloola (Northern Territory). His family are from the Garrawa language group. He has worked as a stockman and a police tracker as well as being employed in land management.

Badger Bates (William Brian Bates) is an Elder of the Paakantji people of north-west New South Wales. His artwork in linoprint, on emu eggs and in wood and stone carving depicts contemporary environmental issues as well as traditional stories. For many years he worked for the National Parks and Wildlife Service.

Betty Lockyer was born in 1942 on Beagle Bay Mission, on the north-west coast of Western Australia. When she was five, her family moved to the pearling town of Broome.

Bob Randall was born in 1934, and spent the first seven years of his life with his Yankunytjatjara family on their traditional land east of Uluru. In 1941 he was Stolen from his family and taken to the institution called the Bungalow, at Alice Springs. Bob is a songwriter and musician.

Bronwyn Penrith was born in 1952 and grew up in Brungle (New South Wales). Since the 1970s she has been an active member of the Aboriginal community of Redfern, where she is now Chair of the Aboriginal women's centre Mudgin-Gal. Recently Bronwyn appeared on television in the role of the Elder, Auntie Bev, in the '2008' episode of the children's television series *My Place*.

Bunthami (I) Yunupingu was an Elder of the Rirratjingu clan. She was responsible for Yalangbara, Yirrkala and the island of Dhambaliya in north-east Arnhem Land (Northern Territory).

Charlotte Phillipus is a Luritja woman who grew up in Papunya (Northern Territory) in the 1950s. The daughter of Western Desert painter, Long Jack Phillipus, Charlotte continues the family art tradition. In the 1990s she was part of the team who developed the Papunya Model of Education.

Daisy Utemorrah was born on Kunmunya Mission in the Kimberley (Western Australia) in 1922. When she was seven she was made to leave her family camp and live in the girls' dormitory. In later life, living in Derby, Daisy became a teacher and linguist. Her picture books for children include *Do Not Go Around the Edges* and *Moonglue*.

Darby Jampijinpa Ross grew up in his traditional Warlpiri homeland in the Central Desert. He later lived in the community of Yuendumu (Northern Territory). A senior Law man, he had responsibility for many *Tjukurrpa* stories and sites, including Flying Ant, Possum, Turkey and Emu. In 2005 he celebrated his 100th birthday.

David Mowaljarli was born in the 1920s at Kunmunya Mission in the Kimberley (Western Australia). A Ngarinyin Law man, he worked on a dictionary and the translation of the Bible into Ngarinyin. He also campaigned for the return of Wanjina peoples to their traditional lands, and was acclaimed as Aboriginal of the Year in 1992.

David Ned David was born in 1966. He was raised on Yam Island, one of the central islands of the Torres Strait, where he still lives. As well as being a singer, composer and dancer, David works for the Australian Quarantine Department.

Deanna McGowan was born in 1962 in the town of Roebourne in the Pilbara region of Western Australia. Her mother is a Kurrama woman. Deanna established the Women's Refuge Centre in Roebourne, while also raising four children. Her interview appeared in the book *Red Dust in her Veins*, which has raised more than $125,000 for the Royal Flying Doctor Service.

Dhuwarrwarr Marika was born in 1946, and lives in the community of Yirrkala (Northern Territory). Like her sister Läklak, she is the daughter of the well-known deceased artist and Elder Mawalan (I) Marika. At the age of twelve, Dhuwarrwarr began learning to paint by helping her father. She is an Elder of the Rirratjingu clan, Dhuwa moiety.

Diane Phillips is a Gunditjmara woman from south-western Victoria. Her mother, Mary Phillips (née King), grew up at Lake Condah Mission. Towards the end of her life, Mary was recognised as NAIDOC Elder of the Year. Diane has passed on her mother's stories to her daughter and grand daughters.

Donna Daly was born in 1959. Until she was ten years old she grew up on the mission at La Perouse, on the shores of Botany Bay, and she still lives in the community. Donna is the administrator of Gujaga MACS child-care centre, which runs language and cultural programs for La Perouse children and families.

Donna Meehan was born in Coonamble (New South Wales) in 1954. At the age of five she was removed from her family and was subsequently raised by a non-Indigenous couple. In the 1980s Donna was reunited with her birth-mother and family. As well as bringing up her children, Donna has worked in various government and community agencies in the Newcastle area.

Don Ross was born in 1915 on his grandfather's pastoral station, Neutral Junction, near Barrow Creek (Northern Territory). His mother was a Kaytetye woman and his father was a white station worker who moved to Queensland soon after Don was born. Don lived with his mother and grandfather and played with the other Kaytetye boys.

Douglas Abbott grew up in the 1950s in the Finke River area (Northern Territory). By this time, the family's traditional land had been turned into pastoral stations, but Douglas's parents retained their links with country by working for the white bosses. Douglas grew up speaking his traditional Arrernte, plus three other Aboriginal languages. He is a well-known artist.

Eileen Alberts is a Gunditjmara woman. She grew up at Little Dunmore, east of Heywood (Victoria), on a small parcel of land bought by her people when they moved off the mission at Lake Condah.

Evelyn Crawford was born near Bourke (New South Wales) in 1928. Like her mother before her, she was a Paakantji woman. After raising a family, Evelyn qualified in the 1970s as an Aboriginal Teachers Aide, and went on to become TAFE Aboriginal Regional Co-ordinator for western New South Wales.

Evelyn Dickerson describes herself as a Noongar girl from Perth. She was born in 1984, and grew up speaking her traditional language, Beeliar, at home. Evelyn was the first Aboriginal girl to do Year 12 at her high school. She won a dance scholarship to Sydney, where she now lives.

Felicia and **Selina** are cousins who live in Broken Hill and go to high school there. They are members of the Spirit Catchers dance group, which is run by the community organisation Thankakali.

Galarrwuy Yunupingu was born in East Arnhem Land in 1948, and attended the mission school at Yirrkala. As one of the senior members of the Gumatj clan, he has taken a leading role in the campaign for Land Rights since the 1960s. Australian of the Year in 1978, Galarrwuy Yunupingu continues to be a spokesperson for his community.

Gapala and **Dharpaloco** have Yolngu family in Yirrkala (Northern Territory) and Darug family in Sydney, where they live. They are members of the contemporary Indigenous dance group, Jannawi.

George Milpurrurru was part of the group of artists from Ramingining (Northern Territory) whose work received recognition across Australia during the 1980s and 1990s. In 1994 he and his fellow artists won a landmark copyright case which established the intellectual property rights of Aboriginal artists.

Gloria Templar was born on Cape Barren Island, Tasmania, in 1941. Together with her cousin, Muriel Maynard, she used to go shell-collecting with their grandmother. A member of the Aboriginal Elders Council of Tasmania, Gloria has been on a number of community committees connected with education, child care and housing.

Goobalathaldin (Dick Roughsey) was a Lardil man, born in 1924 on Mornington Island in the Gulf of Carpentaria. A well-known artist, he collaborated with Percy Tresize on a number of picture books. *The Rainbow Serpent* was Picture Book of the Year in the Children's Book Council of Australia Awards for 1976.

Hazel Brown was born in 1925 in the southern part of Western Australia, where she grew up speaking the language of her Noongar father and stepfather. Hazel's mother was from the Pilbara.

Hilda Muir was born near Borroloola (Northern Territory) in about 1920. Her mother was a Yanyuwa woman and her father was a white man. In 1928 she was taken to the Kahlin Aboriginal Compound in Darwin. In the 1990s Hilda Muir was one of the members of the Stolen Generation who sued the government in the High Court.

Hope Ebsworth was born at Bourke (New South Wales) in 1952, and spent his early years around Wanaaring. His father was a Wangkumarra man from the Channel Country on the border of Queensland and New South Wales.

Hopie Manakgu is from the community of Gunbalunya (Northern Territory). After spending her early childhood in the bush, Hopie felt out of place when she was sent to the mission school. She later went on to do teacher training at Batchelor College, Darwin, in the 1990s.

Ian Abdulla was born at Swan Reach on the River Murray in 1947. His mother was a Ngarrindjeri woman and his father was descended from an Afghan cameleer. Ian's paintings are included in all major public collections around Australia, and his work has also been shown in Spain, The Netherlands, Japan and the United States.

Irene Jimmy grew up during the 1980s with her Gurindji family in the community of Kalkaringi on the Victoria River (Northern Territory). When Irene was still at school, she told her story in the book *My Dreaming is the Christmas Bird*.

Isabel Flick grew up during the 1930s around Collarenebri, in north-west New South Wales. Her father was a Gamilaraay man and her mother was from the neighbouring Bigambul language group. Isabel was famous for 'making trouble' wherever she found racism or injustice. She was awarded a Medal of the Order of Australia in 1986.

Jack Mirritji identified himself as 'Tribe Jinang, Skin Balang, Moiety Dhuwa'. He was born at Warngibimirri in Arnhem Land in about 1930 and grew up in the area around the present-day communities of Millingimbi and Maningrida. In 1972 he recorded his life story for the Literature Centre at Millingimbi School.

Jade is from the Biripi nation. He has grown up in his traditional country near Taree, on the north coast of New South Wales. He was in Year 9 at the time of his interview for this book.

Jaleesa Donovan was born in 1990 and has grown up in the Sydney suburb of Bankstown. The Donovan family is famous in country and western music, and Jaleesa won her first talent quest at the age of four. Her paternal grandparents were Dhanggati and Gumbaynggirr people, of the New South Wales north coast.

Jenny Giles is a Ngarrindjeri/Nganguruku woman from South Australia. She grew up during the 1950s, travelling the Murray River with her family. Jenny still takes every opportunity to revisit the river to fish or hunt. In 1996 she and a friend rowed the River Murray for Reconciliation, from Renmark near the border to Goolwa near the Murray Mouth, a distance of 560 kilometres.

Joe Brown was born in 1948 on Noonkanbah Station in the Kimberley (Western Australia). His language group is Walmajarri and his traditional country is Karningarra, on the Canning Stock Route. Joe is currently a Special Adviser for both the Kimberley Law and Culture Centre and the Kimberley Land Council.

Joshua Booth is an Elder of the Martu people, whose traditional country includes the Pilbara and Percival Lakes area of Western Australia. In 2002 the Martu won recognition as Native Title holders to 136,000 square kilometres of their land.

Jukuna Mona Chaguna, a Walmajarri woman, grew up in the 1950s, when her family was still living a traditional life in the Great Sandy Desert. As an adult she learned to read and write her own language as well as English. Jukuna became a teacher of Walmajarri language and culture in her community at Fitzroy Crossing.

June Barker was born in the 1930s at Cummeragunja Mission, on the banks of the River Murray. Her mother was a Yorta Yorta woman and her father was a Wiradjuri man. By the time June was a teenager she was living at Brewarrina Mission, on the Barwon River in north-west New South Wales, where she later married Roy Barker.

Kain comes from Macksville on the north coast of New South Wales. His language group is Gumbaynggirr. He is interested in following a career in engineering when he finishes school.

Kim Holten was born in Sydney in 1959 and was raised by her grandmother, a Dhanggati woman, in the suburbs of La Perouse and Mascot. After working at the Aboriginal Medical Service, Kim qualified as a teacher. She is currently an Aboriginal Support Officer in the Catholic education system.

Labumore (Elsie Roughsey) was born in 1923 on Goonana Mission, Mornington Island, in the Gulf of Carpentaria. From about the age of seven she was forced to live in the mission dormitory with other girls, but she spent most weekends in the bush with her parents. As a young woman she married Goobalathaldin (Dick Roughsey).

Läklak Marika was born in 1943 in the community of Yirrkala in north-east Arnhem Land. She is an Elder of the Rirratjingu clan, Dhuwa moiety. Like her sister Dhuwarrwarr, she is a well-known artist. Together with other family members she runs land care projects in her community.

Larry Jungarrayi Spencer was born in about 1919 in his traditional Warlpiri country in the Central Desert. In later life, while living in the community of Yuendumu (Northern Territory), he was one of the senior men who painted Law-stories onto the doors of the community school, as a new way of teaching children their culture.

Leah Purcell grew up in Murgon (Queensland) in the 1970s. An award-winning actor, writer, singer and director, Leah has starred in, directed and written iconic Australian films, theatre and television productions such as *Lantana, Jindabyne, Police Rescue, Love My Way, Box the Pony* and *Black Chicks Talking.*

Lena Crabbe grew up in the 1920s in south-west Western Australia. As the eldest of seven children, Lena helped bring up her brothers and sisters.

Lewis Cook is a Bundjalung man. He grew up around the Richmond River, on the north coast of New South Wales.

Linda Burney is of Wiradjuri descent. She was born in 1957 and grew up near Leeton, in the Riverland. After a short time as a classroom teacher, Linda became involved in the Aboriginal Education Consultative Group and later became New South Wales Director-General of Aboriginal Affairs. She is currently a minister in the New South Wales Parliament.

Linda Anderson Tjonggarda was born in Papunya (Northern Territory) in 1962. A Pintupi woman, Linda has a Diploma of Education and has been a teacher at Papunya School since 1990. She was a member of the team who developed the Papunya Model of Education, a bilingual system which balances Indigenous and non-Indigenous ways of learning.

Lola Greeno is a Tasmanian Aboriginal artist. She was born on Cape Barren Island in 1946. When she was twelve, her family moved to Flinders Island. Lola's shell necklaces are held in many major collections, including the National Museum of Australia. As a Program Officer for Aboriginal Arts (Tasmania), Lola runs workshops to train her fellow craftspeople.

Lola James was born in 1941. She traces her Yorta Yorta ancestry back to her great-grandmother Kitty Cooper, a matriarch and midwife. Lola herself is a respected Elder of her community, and took a prominent role during the 1990s in the Yorta Yorta people's campaign for recognition of their Native Title rights.

Lola Young was born in 1942 in the Pilbara (Western Australia), and was taught in the traditional way by her Yinawangka grandfather. Known locally as 'Medicine Woman', Lola knows a great deal about using bush plants for healing. She passes on her wisdom in educational bush walks.

Margaret Tucker was born in 1904, and grew up with her family on Cummeragunja Mission, on the New South Wales side of the Murray River. At the age of thirteen, she was forcibly taken to Cootamundra Girls Training School. In the 1960s, Margaret became one of the founders of the United Council of Aboriginal and Islander Women.

Marrnyula Mununggurr was born in 1964. A member of the Dhuwa moiety of the Djapu clan, her homeland is at Wandawuy in north-east Arnhem Land (Northern Territory). Her art was included in the Saltwater Collection (1999), which toured major Australian galleries in support of the Yolngu claim for the recognition of their sea rights.

Mary Malbunka was born at Haasts Bluff (Northern Territory) in 1959. A Pintupi/Luritja woman, she grew up at Papunya in the family of her cousin, Charlotte Phillipus. In 2003 she published her picture book memoir, *When I Was Little, like You.*

Matt lives in south-west Sydney, where his Wiradjuri mother also grew up. Matt was completing Year 12 at the time of his interview.

Mayrah Sonter is a Wiradjuri woman. She was born in 1983 and grew up in Redfern, in inner Sydney. As Head of Events at Vibe Australia, an Indigenous media, communications and events agency, she organises events such as the Vibe 3on3® and Vibe Alive festivals, and the annual Deadly Awards.

Mick Namerari Tjapaltjarri was born in about 1927 in his traditional Pintupi country in the Western Desert. After working as a stockman, Mick moved to the community of Papunya (Northern Territory) where in 1971 he became one of the founders of Papunya Tula Artists.

Molly Mallett (née Maynard) is descended from Mannalargenna, leader of Tasmania's Cape Portland tribe. She was born on Cape Barren Island in 1926, but moved to Launceston when she was a teenager. Molly worked for the Tasmanian Aboriginal Education Council for many years.

Molly Nungarrayi grew up during the 1930s in her traditional country around the Lander River (Northern Territory). A senior Warlpiri woman, she later lived in the community of Wirliyajarrayi.

Morndi Munro was born in about 1909 in the Kimberley. A member of the Unggumi language group, Morndi grew up around Derby, Fitzroy Crossing and Wyndham (Western Australia).

Muriel Maynard was born on Cape Barren Island in 1937. Muriel's great-great-grandmother, Nimarena, was one of the Aboriginal people taken to the Wybelena settlement on Flinders Island in the 1800s. Muriel continues the tradition of shell-necklace making passed down by her grandmother.

Naminapu Maymaru was born in the north-east Arnhem Land community of Yirrkala in 1952. Like other members of her family, she is well-known for her traditional bark paintings. As well as working as a teacher at Yirrkala School, Naminapu has been the curator of the art museum in her community.

Nicole spent her childhood in the New South Wales town of Walgett. Now enrolled at a Sydney boarding school, Nicole goes back to Walgett for holidays with family and friends.

Olive Jackson was born in 1930. Her mother was a Yorta Yorta woman and her father was Wiradjuri. Olive worked for the Aborigines Advancement League for many years, as well as raising nine children.

Oodgeroo Noonuccal (Kath Walker) was born in 1920 on Stradbroke Island, across the water from Brisbane. A highly acclaimed poet, Oodgeroo's publications include the children's book *Stradbroke Dreamtime*. She was appointed a member of the Order of the British Empire in 1970 but in 1988 she returned the medal as a protest against the Bicentenary celebrations.

Paddy Japaljarri Stewart grew up in the Central Desert during the 1920s. A Warlpiri man, he was a senior member of the community at Yuendumu, and was one of the Elders who painted traditional stories on the Yuendumu school doors. In 1989 he travelled to Paris to create a sand painting at the Centre Georges Pompidou.

Patricia Lee Napangarti was born in 1960 and grew up in her traditional country near the community of Balgo (Western Australia). Like her older relative Tjama Freda Napanangka, Patricia is a Kukatja Law woman and artist.

Peggy Patrick, Mona Ramsay and **Shirley Purdie** grew up in the 1930s and 1940s in their Kija homeland in the East Kimberley (Western Australia). In later life they became senior members of Warmun Aboriginal Community.

Peter Skipper was born in 1929 in the Great Sandy Desert (Western Australia) and grew up in a traditional way on Walmajarri land. Since the 1960s, he has lived at Fitzroy Crossing, and has been involved in the production of the Walmajarri dictionary and Bible.

Punata Stockman was born in 1956 in the community of Haasts Bluff (Northern Territory). She was the eldest child of Billy Stockman Tjapaltjarri, one of the founders of Papunya Tula. A former teacher at Papunya School, Punata is currently Chair of the Papunya Tjupi Arts Centre.

Rankin Deveraux was born in 1977 in his traditional Mak Mak country. He is part-owner of Deveraux Stock and Station Contractors – a family partnership based on country and involved in breeding Bazadaise-cross cattle. He notes: 'I would like to acknowledge all the people past and present from Meneling Station, Northern Territory, for enriching my early childhood. *Pulum.*'

Raymond Ingrey was born in 1982 and grew up in the La Perouse Aboriginal community. His language group is Dharawal. As a youngster, Ray attended Gujaga preschool, where he now facilitates language and cultural programs for the next generation of La Perouse children.

Ricky is a young Gumbaynggirr man. His traditional country is on the north coast of New South Wales. Since Year 2 he has been learning his language with the help of local Elders. He is currently enrolled at a Sydney boarding school.

Rininya divides her time between a Sydney boarding school and the Riverland town of Griffith, where she lives with her mother, grandmother and great-grandmother. One of Rininya's dreams is to see an Aboriginal woman as Prime Minister of Australia.

Rita Huggins was born in 1921 in the land of the Bidjara-Pitjara people, in north Queensland, but she grew up on the government reserve at Cherbourg, where the so-called Aborigines Protection Act effectively made the residents into prisoners. In the 1960s, Rita became active in her community. She contributed greatly to the life of the community in Brisbane.

Roy Kebisu was born in 1962 and grew up on Yam Island, in the Torres Strait. He proudly claims his descent from Chief Kebisu from Warrior Island (Tudu). In 2007 he was Deputy Council Chairman of his island community. He is trying to engage young people in the traditional songs and dances.

Ronnie Mason grew up during the 1950s on the New South Wales south coast, where he and his family still live on their traditional country. In recent years the family have been campaigning for legal recognition of their ancestral fishing rights.

Russell Mullett was born in 1952. He grew up with his eleven brothers and sisters at the community of Jacksons Track (Victoria), where his parents had settled in order to escape from the repression of the reserve at Lake Tyers.

Sandy Atkinson was born on Cummeragunja Mission in 1932. A Moidaban man, he was one of the founders of the Shepparton Keeping Place. Sandy has also played a significant role in the Koorie Heritage Trust, and is a former Chair of the Aboriginal and Torres Strait Islander Arts Board of the Australia Council.

Sheridan is from the Biripi nation. She has grown up near Taree on the mid north coast of New South Wales. At the time of her interview she was enrolled at a Sydney boarding school.

Shirley Smith became known across Australia as 'MumShirl'. Of Wiradjuri descent, she was raised in the 1920s at Erambie Mission (New South Wales) but spent her adult life in the Sydney suburb of Redfern. A founding member of the Aboriginal Legal Service and Medical Service, she was voted Aborigine of the Year in 1990.

Tamara, **Amelia** and **Deborah** come from Walgett, in north-west New South Wales. Their language group is Gamilaraay. At the time of their interview they were all enrolled at a Sydney boarding school.

Tess Napaljarri Ross is a Warlpiri Elder from Yuendumu (Northern Territory). When traditional Law was painted onto the doors at Yuendumu School in the 1980s, Tess translated the documentation of the Law-stories from Warlpiri into English. The Yuendumu Doors later travelled to art galleries around Australia.

Thompson Yulidjirri was born around 1930 and grew up at Gunbalunya (Northern Territory). A respected artist and ceremonial Elder, his bark paintings are held in major Australian collections. He was also one of the choreographers of the Aboriginal dance performed at the Sydney 2000 Olympic Games Opening Ceremony.

Tjama Freda Napanangka was born out bush in her traditional Kukatja country in the Great Sandy Desert (Western Australia) during the 1930s. In recent years she has lived in the community of Balgo, where she is a senior Law woman and a custodian of her country.

Tjimarri Sanderson-Milera was born in 1993 in South Australia, and is from the Kukatha, Narrunga and Adnyamathanha language groups. A student, actor, athlete and dancer, Tjimarri's main sport is surf lifesaving. He competes in local, state and national competitions, with a silver medal win at the Australian Titles in 2009. That same year he was named NAIDOC Sportsperson of the Year in South Australia.

Tom Calma is an Elder from the Kungarakan and the Iwaidja language groups (Northern Territory). From 2004 until 2009 he was Aboriginal and Torres Strait Islander Social Justice Commissioner and national Race Discrimination Commissioner for the Human Rights and Equal Opportunities Commission.

Tommy George is an Elder of the Taipan clan. He grew up in his traditional country on Cape York (Queensland). Together with Dr George Musgrave, he founded the biennial Laura Festival of traditional dance and culture. In 2005 he was awarded an honorary Doctorate of Letters by James Cook University for his ecological expertise.

Tommy Kngwarraye Thompson is a Kaytetye Elder. As a traditional owner for Rtwerrpe country, including Artarre community, in Central Australia, he has assisted many Native Title claims. Tommy is a renowned storyteller and plays an active role in education, through traditional ceremony and also by working with Neutral Junction school and producing media such as books and films.

Troy and **Geoffrey** are cousins. They come from Walgett, in north-west New South Wales, and proudly identify as Gamilaraay. They enjoy playing football (preferably rugby league) and spending time with family.

Vivienne Mason is a Yuin woman from the south coast of New South Wales. Growing up during the 1950s, she learned traditional knowledge about the sea and fishing. A local Traditional Owner and Elder of the south coast, Vivienne is currently Chair of the Wagonga Local Aboriginal Land Council. She is campaigning for the right for her people to hunt and gather seafood, unrestrained by rules and licence fees.

Wandjuk Marika was born in about 1927 in East Arnhem Land (Northern Territory). His father was a leader of the Rirratjingu clan, and Wandjuk in turn became clan leader. Wandjuk Marika was also famous as an artist, composer, writer and Land Rights activist. He was one of the founders of the Aboriginal Arts Board of the Australia Council.

Wenten Rubuntja, an Arrernte man, was born in the Alice Springs area in the mid 1920s. Although he mostly grew up in the town camps along the Todd River, he had a very traditional education. In the 1980s Wenten played a leading role in setting up Yipirinya, an independent Aboriginal school that promotes two-way learning.

Yami Lester, a Yankunytjatjara man, was born in about 1941. When he was twelve years old he suddenly went blind when the British nuclear testing took place near his home at Emu Field (South Australia). Yami played a major role in the fight for the hand-back of Uluru, and in gaining recognition for Aboriginal people affected by the atomic tests at Maralinga.

Acknowledgements and bibliography

Contributors are listed alphabetically, by first name. Those under the age of eighteen at the time of interview are listed by first name only. Page numbers are noted after contributors' names.

All contributors retain copyright over their own words. We have undertaken a lengthy permissions process, and have tried in each case to secure the permission of the Aboriginal or Torres Strait Islander contributor or an appropriate family member. If we have inadvertently missed someone, we apologise. Please let us know, so that we can make the correct acknowledgement in the next edition of this book.

Abbreviations
ACES: Aboriginal Community Elders Service
AIATSIS: Australian Institute of Aboriginal and Torres Strait Islander Studies
et al.: and others
op cit.: work already cited

Text

Alice Bilari Smith (14, 63, 83): Alice Smith with Anna Vitenbergs & Loreen Brehaut, *Under a bilari tree I born: the story of Alice Bilari Smith*, Fremantle Arts Centre Press, Fremantle, 2002.
Alice Nannup (14): Alice Nannup et al., *When the pelican laughed*, Fremantle Arts Centre Press, South Fremantle, 1992.
Alice Rigney (17): in Virginia Gill, ed., *Leading from the edge: Aboriginal educational leaders tell their story*, South Australian Centre for Leaders in Education, Hindmarsh, 2008, © Commonwealth of Australia.
Andy Tjilari (31, 49): Andy Tjilari, originally recorded & translated by Bill Edwards; adapted by Sandra Ken & Audrey Brumby, *Learning as a Pitjantjatjara child: an Andy Tjilari story,* Anangu Education Services, Northgate, 2006.
Arone Meeks (79): *Koori Mail*, 29 February 2009.
Arthur Shadforth (7): in Fiona Walsh & Paul Mitchell, eds, *Planning for country*, IAD Press, Alice Springs, 2002.
Betty Lockyer (47, 70): Betty Lockyer, 'War Baby', in *Holding up the sky: Aboriginal women speak*, Magabala Books, Broome, 1999.
Bob Randall (19, 52): Bob Randall, *Songman: the story of an Aboriginal Elder of Uluru*, ABC Books, a division of Harper Collins Publishers Australia, Sydney, 2003.

Bunthami (I) Yunupingu (46): in Peter McConchie, 'Gathering', *Elders: wisdom from Australia's Indigenous leaders*, Cambridge University Press, Melbourne, 2003.
Charlotte Phillipus (7): The Papunya Curriculum Project, Papunya School, 1999.
Daisy Utemorrah (29): in Jennifer Isaacs, ed., *Australian Dreaming: 40,000 years of Aboriginal history*, Lansdowne Press, Sydney, 1980. With permission of the family.
Darby Jampijinpa Ross (42, 72): in Liam Campbell, *Darby: one hundred years of life in a changing culture*, ABC Books & Warlpiri Media Association, Sydney, 2006.
David Mowaljarli (83): in Stuart Rintoul, *The wailing: a national black oral history*, William Heinemann, Port Melbourne, 1993. With permission of the family.
David Ned David (74): Ned David, William Kepa & Karl William Neuenfeldt, *Ned David interviewed by William Kepa and Karl Neuenfeldt in the Torres Strait songs project*, ORAL TRC 5728/7, National Library of Australia, 2007.
Deanna McGowan (39): in Lisa Holland-McNair with Melva Stone OAM & Erica Smyth, *Red dust in her veins: women of the Pilbara*, UWA Publishing, Crawley, 2007.
Diane Phillips (43): in ACES & Kate Harvey, *Aboriginal Elders' voices: stories of the 'Tide of history'*, Victorian Indigenous Elders' life stories & oral histories, ACES & Language Australia, Melbourne, 2003.
Don Ross (62): Alexander Donald Pwerle Ross & Terry Whitebeach, *The versatile man: the life and times of Don Ross, Kaytetye stockman*, IAD Press, Alice Springs, 2007.
Donna Meehan (15): in Doreen Mellor & Anna Haebich, eds, *Many voices: reflections on experiences of Indigenous child separation*, National Library of Australia, Canberra, 2002; Donna Meehan, *It's no secret*, Random House, Sydney, 2000.
Douglas Abbott (10, 49): in Stuart Rintoul, op. cit.
Eileen Alberts (50): in ACES & Kate Harvey, op. cit.
Evelyn Crawford (31, 51): Evelyn Crawford as told to Chris Walsh, *Over my tracks*, Penguin Group (Australia), Ringwood, 1993.
Galarrwuy Yunupingu (39): Galarrwuy Yunupingu, Peter Read & Jackie Huggins, *Galarrwuy Yunupingu interviewed by Jackie Huggins and Peter Read in the Australians of the year oral history project*, ORAL TRC 4604, National Library of Australia, 2000.
George Milpurrurru (75): in Penny Tweedie, *Aboriginal Australians: spirit of Arnhem Land*, New Holland, Frenchs Forest, 1998.

Gloria Templar (17, 32): in Tasmania Department of Education, *As I remember: recollections of Aboriginal people*, Gloria Templar & Muriel Maynard interviewed by Lola Greeno, Department of Education, Hobart, 2000.
Goobalathaldin (Dick Roughsey) (9, 55): Dick Roughsey (Goobalathaldin), *Moon and rainbow: the autobiography of an Aboriginal*, Reed, Sydney, 1971. With permission of the family.
Hazel Brown (31, 37, 43): Kim Scott & Hazel Brown, *Kayang & me*, Fremantle Arts Centre Press, Fremantle, 2005.
Hilda Muir (14, 57): Hilda Jarman Muir, *Very big journey: my life as I remember it*, Aboriginal Studies Press, Canberra, 2004.
Hope Ebsworth (53): Hope Ebsworth, *Bury me at Tartulla Hill*, Keeaira Press, Southport, 2009.
Hopie Manakgu (38): in Batchelor College, *Ngoonjook: Batchelor journal of Aboriginal education*, September 1991. With permission of the family.
Ian Abdulla (47, 63): Ian Abdulla, *As I grew older: the life and times of a Nunga growing up along the River Murray*, Omnibus Books, Norwood, 1993.
Irene Jimmy (58, 70): Sarah Fitzherbert, *My Dreaming is the Christmas bird: the story of Irene Jimmy*, Bookshelf Publishing Australia, Melbourne, 1989. With permission of the family.
Isabel Flick (21, 66): Isabel Flick & Heather Goodall, *Isabel Flick: the many lives of an extraordinary Aboriginal woman*, Allen & Unwin, Crows Nest, 2004.
Jack Mirritji (20, 41, 83): Jack Mirritji, *My people's life: An Aboriginal's own story*, Milingimbi Literature Centre, Milingimbi, 1978. With permission of the family.
Jenny Giles (39): in Adele Pring, ed., *Women of the Centre*, Pascoe Publishing, Apollo Bay, 1990.
Joe Brown (7): in Kimberley Aboriginal Law and Culture Centre, *Yirra: land, law and language – strong and alive*, Kimberley Aboriginal Law and Culture Centre, Fitzroy Crossing, 1996.
Joshua Booth (9): in Megan Lewis, *Conversations with the mob*, UWA Publishing, Crawley, 2008.
Jukuna Mona Chaguna (9, 30, 52): in Ngarta Jinny Bent et al., *Two sisters: Ngarta & Jukuna*, Fremantle Arts Centre Press, Fremantle, 2003.

June Barker (69): in Cilka Zagar, *Goodbye riverbank: the Barwon–Namoi people tell their story*, Magabala Books, Broome, 2000.

Labumore (Elsie Roughsey) (11): Labumore, edited by Paul Memmott & Robyn Horsman, *An Aboriginal mother tells of the old and the new*, McPhee Gribble–Penguin Books, Fitzroy, 1984.

Läklak Marika (8): in Gillian Hutcherson, *Gong-wapitja: women and art from Yirrkala, northeast Arnhem Land*, Aboriginal Studies Press, Canberra, 1998; **(46):** in Peter McConchie, op. cit.

Lena Crabbe (62): in Sally Morgan et al., *Speaking from the heart: stories of life, family and country*, Fremantle Arts Centre Press, Fremantle, 2007.

Lewis Cook (56): in Jennifer Hoff, *Bundjalung Jugun = Bundjalung country*, Richmond River Historical Society, Lismore, 2006.

Lola Greeno (32): Lola Greeno & Gwenda Davey, *Lola Greeno interviewed by Gwenda Davey in the Tradition bearers oral history project*, ORAL TRC 5032/17, National Library of Australia, 2004.

Lola James (17, 87): in ACES & Kate Harvey, op. cit.

Lola Young (41): in Lola Young with Anna Vitenbergs, *Lola Young: medicine woman and teacher*, Fremantle Arts Centre Press, Fremantle, 2007.

Margaret Tucker (37, 44, 66): Margaret Tucker, *If everyone cared*, Grosvenor, London, 1983.

Mary Malbunka (11, 44, 51): Mary Malbunka, *When I was little, like you*, Allen & Unwin, Crows Nest, 2003.

Molly Mallett (37): Molly Mallett, *My past – their future: stories from Cape Barren Island*, Blubber Head Press in association with Riawunna, Centre for Aboriginal Education, Sandy Bay, 2001.

Molly Nungarrayi (86): in Molly Nungarrayi et al., compiled and edited by Petronella Vaarzon-Morel, *Warlpiri karnta karnta-kurlangu yimi = Warlpiri women's voices: our lives, our history*, IAD Press, Alice Springs, 1995.

Morndi Munro (29, 49): Morndi Munro, edited by Mary Anne Jebb, *Emerarra: a man of Merarra*, Magabala Books, Broome, 1996.

Muriel Maynard (32): in Tasmania Department of Education, op cit.

Naminapu Maymaru (78): in Gillian Hutcherson, op. cit.

Olive Jackson (52, 77): in ACES & Kate Harvey, op. cit. With permission of the family.

Oodgeroo Noonuccal (50, 56): Oodgeroo Noonuccal, *Stradbroke Dreamtime*, Angus & Robertson, Pymble, 1999.

Paddy Japaljarri Stewart (77): Paddy Japaljarri Stewart, translated by Sarah Napaljarri Ross, tape transcription Warlpiri Media Association, Yuendumu, 1991, courtesy of Warlukurlangu Artists Aboriginal Association, in David Horton & AIATSIS, *The encyclopaedia of Aboriginal Australia*, Aboriginal Studies Press, Canberra, 1994.

Patricia Lee Napangarti (12): in Tjama Freda Napanangka et al., compiled and edited by Sonja Peter & Pamela Lofts, *Yarrtji: six women's stories from the Great Sandy Desert*, Aboriginal Studies Press, Canberra, 1997.

Peggy Patrick, Mona Ramsay & Shirley Purdie (10): in Margaret Stewart, ed., *Ngalangangpum Jarrakpu Purrurn = Mother and child: the women of Warmun as told to Margaret Stewart*, Magabala Books, Broome, 1999.

Peter Skipper (64): in Honey Bulugardie et al., edited by Eirlys Richards et al., *Out of the desert: stories from the Walmajarri exodus*, Magabala Books, Broome, 2002.

Rankin Deveraux (8): in Deborah Bird Rose in collaboration with Sharon D'Amico et al., *Country of the heart: an Indigenous Australian homeland*, Aboriginal Studies Press, Canberra, 2002.

Rita Huggins (20, 69): Rita Huggins & Jackie Huggins, *Auntie Rita*, Aboriginal Studies Press, Canberra, 1994.

Ronnie Mason (53): in Susan Dale Donaldson, researcher, *Stories about the Eurobodalla by Aboriginal people*, public report, Eurobodalla Shire Council, Moruya, 2006.

Roy Kebisu (28, 74): Roy Kebisu & Karl William Neuenfeldt, *Roy Kebisu interviewed by Karl Neuenfeldt in the Torres Strait songs project*, ORAL TRC 5728/8, National Library of Australia, 2007.

Russell Mullett (21): in Alick Jackomos & Derek Fowell, *Living Aboriginal history of Victoria: stories in the oral tradition*, Cambridge University Press, Melbourne, 1991.

Sandy Atkinson (58, 69): in Mission voices: hear our stories, 'Voices of Cummeragunja', © Australian Broadcasting Corporation, Film Victoria and Koorie Heritage Trust Inc. 2004, http://www.abc.net.au/missionvoices/cummeragunja/voices_of_cummerangunja/default.htm

Shirley Smith (38): Colleen Shirley Perry, with the assistance of Bobbi Sykes, *MumShirl: an autobiography*, Heinemann Education, Richmond, 1987.

Tess Napaljarri Ross (78): in Warlukurlangu Artists, *Yuendumu doors*, Aboriginal Studies Press, Canberra, 1987, courtesy of Warlukurlangu Artists Aboriginal Association.

Tjama Freda Napanangka (13): in Tjama Freda Napanangka et al., op. cit.

Tjimarri Sanderson-Milera (67): *Koori Mail*, 8 September 2010.

Tom Calma (87): speech, Yabun Festival, Victoria Park, Sydney, 26 January 2010.

Tommy George (75): in Peter McConchie, 'Ceremony and song', op. cit.

Tommy Kngwarraye Thompson (61, 64): Tommy Kngwarraye Thompson, compiled by Myfany Turpin, *Growing up Kaytetye: stories*, Jukurrpa Books, Alice Springs, 2003.

Vivienne Mason (56): in Susan Dale Donaldson, op. cit.

Wandjuk Marika (33, 83): Wandjuk Marika, *Wandjuk Marika: life story*, as told to Jennifer Isaacs, UQP, St Lucia, 1995.

Wenten Rubuntja (9, 11, 73): Wenten Rubuntja with Jenny Green, *The town grew up dancing: the life and art of Wenten Rubuntja*, Jukurrpa Books, Alice Springs, 2002.

Yami Lester (45, 77): Yami Lester, *Yami: the autobiography of Yami Lester*, IAD Press, Alice Springs, 2000; **(30, 51):** Yami Lester, edited by Petronella Vaarzon-Morel, *Learning from the land*, IAD Press, Alice Springs, 1995.

The following people, interviewed by Nadia Wheatley, also retain copyright in their own words: **Amelia (61), Andrew (16, 64), Bronwyn Penrith (29, 80), Charlotte Phillipus (40), Deborah (61), Dharpaloco (73), Donna Daly (26), Evelyn Dickerson (27), Felicia (75), Gapala (73), Geoffrey (47), Jade (84), Jaleesa Donovan (81), Kain (63), Kim Holten (71, 79), Leah Purcell (16, 80), Linda Burney (35, 85), Linda Anderson Tjonggarda (22, 25), Matt (64, 77), Mayrah Sonter (67, 85), Nicole (59), Raymond Ingrey (26, 87), Ricky (27, 84), Rininya (23), Selina (75), Sheridan (34), Tamara (61),** and **Troy (47).**

Thanks to the many schools and community organisations who helped us, especially Aboriginal Community Elders Service, Ara Irititja Project, Gujaga MACS, Broken Hill High School, Kapululangu Women's Law and Culture Centre, Kimberley Aboriginal Law and Culture Centre, Mirndiyan Gununa Aboriginal Corporation, Mowanjum Artists Spirit of the Wandjina Aboriginal Corporation, Presbyterian Ladies College (Sydney), St Joseph's College, St Scholastica's College, Wagonga Local Aboriginal Land Council, Warlayirti Artists and Warlukurlangu Artists Aboriginal Association.

Acknowledgements continued

Images

As with text, copyright in art and photographs is retained by original copyright holders, whether or not it is marked ©.

Illustrations throughout © Ken Searle.
8: Sharon D'Amico, from Deborah Bird Rose, op.cit.
9: Erwin Chlanda, *Alice Springs News,* 25 October 2000.
10: Penny Tweedie, <http://pennytweedie.com/>.
11: Baldwin Spencer, reproduced courtesy Museum Victoria, XP9549.
13: Dhuwarrwarr Marika, 'The Djangkawu give birth', ochres on bark, 114 x 70 cm, 1991, reproduced courtesy of National Museum of Ethnology, Japan. Photograph by the National Museum.
14: Papunya School Publishing Committee.
15: Justin McManus / Fairfax Photos.
16: Axel Poignant, 'Mangawila and his boys gather around to make camp, Liverpool River, September 1952', from Roslyn Poignant with Axel Poignant, *Encounter at Nagalarramba*, National Library of Australia, Canberra, 1996, image supplied by National Library of Australia, nlapic-vn4978576.
21: Richard Seeger, reproduced courtesy Museum Victoria, XP3495.
23: Badger Bates, 'Mission Mob and Bend Mob, Wilcannia 1950s', linocut print, 73 x 43 cm, image © and courtesy the artist, Museum of Contemporary Art, purchased with funds provided by the Coe and Mordant families, 2009.
24: Penny Tweedie.
26–7: Nadia Wheatley, with permission from Gujaga MACS families.
27: Nadia Wheatley.
28: © Belinda Wright / Lochman Transparencies.
29: Axel Poignant, 'Mamerirrnginj and her child, Liverpool River Region, Northern Territory, 1952', from Roslyn Poignant with Axel Poignant, op. cit., image supplied by National Library of Australia, nla.pic-vn4439006.
30–1: Image courtesy of the State Library of South Australia, SLSA: PRG 214/45/B96 JRB Love collection, 'Man showing group of children how to make Miru', 1937.

32: Vanessa Greeno, from Amanda Jane Reynolds, ed., *Keeping culture: Aboriginal Tasmania*, National Museum of Australia Press, Canberra, 2006.
34: Heide Smith, <http://www.heidesmith.com/default.html>.
35: photo Jennifer Isaacs, <http://www.jenniferisaacs.com.au/>.
36: Richard Seeger, reproduced courtesy Museum Victoria, XP3660.
38: Punata Stockman, from workshop with Nadia Wheatley, Papunya School, 2000.
40: Ken Searle.
41: Christine Howes, © Koori Mail, from *Koori Mail*, 22 April 2009.
43: Mick Namerari Tjapaltjarri, 'Naughty Boys' Dreaming', 1971, © estate of the artist 2010, licensed by Aboriginal Artists Agency Ltd; explanatory drawing by Frank Slip and Geoffrey Bardon, from Geoffrey Bardon & James Bardon, *Papunya: a place made after the story: the beginnings of the Western Desert painting movement*, Melbourne University Publishing, Carlton, 2004.
44: Mary Malbunka, © estate of the artist.
45: © Stanley Breeden / Lochman Transparencies.
46: photo Jennifer Isaacs.
49: Penny Tweedie.
50: Ken Searle.
51: photo © Pamela Lofts, 1997, from Tjama Freda Napanangka et al., op. cit.
52: Joan Haynes, image supplied by AIATSIS, AIATSIS.199.BW – N4806.22.
53: Megan Lewis, reproduced with permission of UWA Publishing.
55: Paul Wright, <http://www.paulwright.com.au/>.
56: photo Jennifer Isaacs.
57: Marrnyula Mununggurr, 'Living by the sea', ochres on bark, 111 x 96 cm, from *Saltwater: Yirrkala bark paintings of sea country*, Buku-Larrnngay Mulka Centre in association with Jennifer Isaacs Publishing, 1999.
58: Howard Birnstihl, <http://www.ozimages.com.au/PWS.asp?MemberID=1487>.
59: Nicole.
60: photograph by D. F. Thomson, courtesy of Thomson family and Museum Victoria, TPH 4124.
61: Tamara.
62 (left): Larry Jungarrayi Spencer, courtesy of Warlukurlangu Artists Aboriginal Association.

62 (right): photograph by D. F. Thomson, courtesy of the Thomson family and Museum Victoria, TPH 1250.
63 (left): Richard Baker.
63 (right): Jon Altman, image supplied by AIATSIS, Altman.J1.CS – 69804.
65: Ian Abdulla, image courtesy of the artist and Andrew Fox.
66 (top): Heide Smith.
66 (bottom) and 67: © Andrew Rosenfeldt, from Vibe 3on3®.
68: Penny Tweedie.
69: © Newspix / Neville Whitmarsh. With permission of the Perkins family.
70: Ken Searle.
72–3: Darren Coyne, © Koori Mail, from *Koori Mail*, 11 February 2009.
74: Kirstie Parker, © Koori Mail, from *Koori Mail*, 17 June 2009.
75: Thompson Yulidjirri, Kunwinjku, born 1930, 'Wubarr ceremony', 1989, earth pigments on stringybark, 171.3 x 73.7 cm, National Gallery of Victoria, Melbourne, © estate of the artist, 2010, licensed by Aboriginal Artists Agency Ltd, purchased through The Art Foundation of Victoria with the assistance of Pacific Dunlop Limited, Fellow, 1990.
76–7: Photo Steve Strike; caption text © Uluru-Kata Tjuta National Park. Both from 'The creation period' in <http://www.environment.gov.au/parks/uluru/culture-history/culture/creation.html>.
78 (top left): Nadia Wheatley, reproduced with permission of Elder Jacko Smith.
78 (bottom left): Ute Eickelkamp, image supplied by AIATSIS, U1.CS – 118343.
78 (right): Peter Los, from Vivien Johnson, *Clifford Possum Tjapaltjarri*, Art Gallery of South Australia, Adelaide, 2003.
79: Christine Howes, © Koori Mail, from *Koori Mail*, 29 February, 2009.
80: Courtesy of Jabal Films Pty Ltd, from the collection of The National Film and Sound Archive.
81: Nadia Wheatley.
82: Penny Tweedie.
84: Graham Hunt, © Koori Mail, from *Koori Mail*, 15 July 2009.
85: Heide Smith.

Glossary

Country: When Aboriginal people refer to 'my country', they mean the area that is the traditional homeland of their language group. This country comprises all the plants and creatures and people who have lived in that area since the beginning of time. As well, it is the soil and the water and the sky overhead.

Language group, nation: Most linguists agree that when Europeans arrived in Australia, there were at least 250 languages being spoken on the continent, and as many dialects. People who spoke a particular language all belonged to the same homeland or country.

These days, the terms 'language group' or 'nation' are often used instead of the old anthropological term 'tribe'. Even if Aboriginal people today no longer speak their language or live in their homeland, they still usually identify as belonging to their language group and to their traditional country.

Law: In traditional Aboriginal society, specific laws about people's behaviour and laws governing the ecosystem are held together inside one Law, which is seen as having existed from Creation up to the present day. Different words for the Law are used in different languages. These include *Tjukurrpa, Jukurrpa, Ngarrangkarni* and *Jukurtani*. (In English, these words are sometimes translated as 'the Dreamtime' or 'the Dreaming'.)

The Law is passed on through oral history, art and ceremony.

Oral history: This means history that is initially spoken, rather than history that begins as a written text. Many of us, whatever our cultural backgrounds, grow up hearing oral histories from our parents and grandparents. Sometimes, oral history is spoken into a tape recorder, and then the words are written down and published in a book – such as this one. Aboriginal people have been passing on oral history for many thousands of years. In recent years many Aboriginal people have also published their oral histories in books.

Skin, skin group, right skin: 'Skin' is a term used by anthropologists to describe the additional set of family relationships that Aboriginal people traditionally have. It has nothing to do with the colour of people's skin.

Index

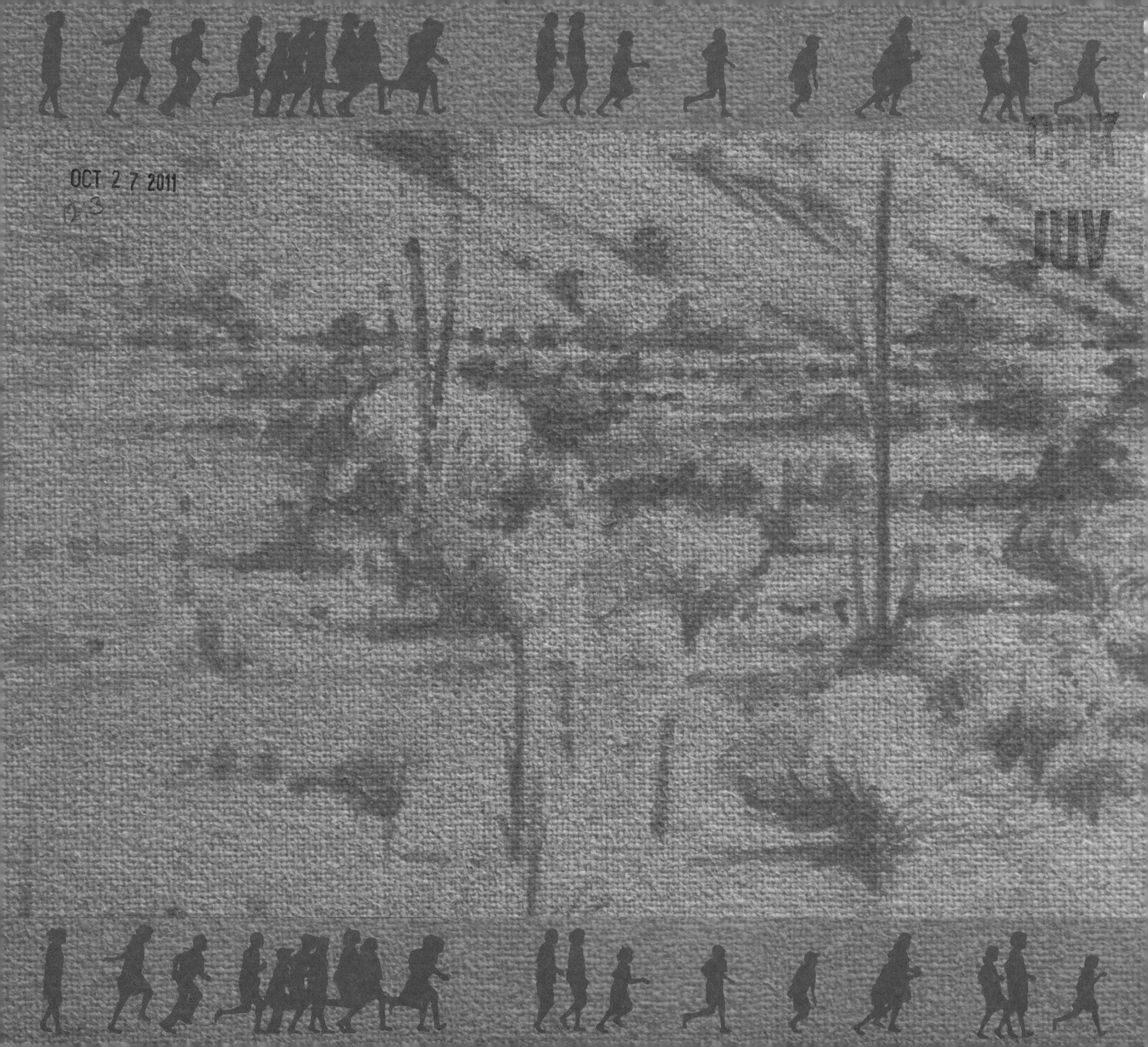